Thelma's People

*A year during the time of The Troubles
in Northern Ireland*

by
Pat McEniff
and Marita Mulcahy

ISBN 978-0-9566222-0-4

Printed by Browne Printers Ltd
Letterkenny +353749121387

I

It was as soft day in Sydare outside Ballinacurlew the Friday before Mothers' Day in 1982. Sydare, a mainly Protestant townland, was full of upright, hard-working farmers. They had little or no borrowings from banks – what they couldn't afford they wouldn't have – and they went out of their way to avoid scandals of any sort. It was a hilly area of good land 'and the odd horse grazed quietly amongst herds of fat cattle. It was a place one could comfortably call home.

The daffodils danced in the Spring breeze – the daffodils that Olive Elliot had set two years ago. Albert, her husband, had just gone to pick some for her. She was waiting to arrange them in the jug with the long neck when he returned. She smiled as she drew the cool water from the tap in the scullery and added the aspirin so that the flowers would last longer. She knew that he would tease her. He always said that cut flowers were not meant to last. It would be seven days before these were thrown out – seven days during which her life would be changed forever.

* * *

It was nine o'clock, and Albert wasn't due in Kitchiner's Barracks until ten. He straightened himself as he looked in the mirror, pulling on his Ulster Defence Regiment beret and tilting it to one side. He was forty-six, fairly tall and dark-haired, had brown eyes and was handsome, yet he always wished he was as tall as his brother Robert. He was four inches smaller at five foot ten, but even then he considered himself not such a bad figure of a man and his uniform was quite well filled out. He buttoned his belt and unlocked the cupboard door. His Browning glistened. He had spent half an hour cleaning, checking and oiling it just before he went to bed the previous night. He was quietly proud that his Sergeant Major always said that he was the best-turned-out and most able man in the Company. This resulted in his recently being promoted to Corporal, First Class. His new red stripe and medal said everything and compounded his feeling of pride. He enthusiasm made him take the stairs to the big bedroom two steps at a time so that he could quickly check the stock from the window there. He never resisted the urge to look out the window of that room. The view of the near field and the haggard gave him a comfortable feeling. The Charolais cattle were all there, backside into the breeze. He marvelled at how well they had adapted to Fermanagh with its drumlins as opposed to the flat fields of France. They stood tall on the ground – their bellies well up from the rushes in the low- lying area in which they grazed. He also looked fondly at his brood mare, Bobbin. She was sleek, dark brown and elegant – a direct descendant of his father's beautiful old mare, Mollie, who had won many a red ribbon at the Balmoral Show. She was fairly close to foaling and looked huge and content.

Racing downstairs and outside onto the gravel, he shoved a clip in the Browning for safety. He unlocked and opened the boot and the bonnet of his red Ford Capri. As usual, he checked it thoroughly in case it might have been tampered with. Manoeuvres were to be at Belcoo that day and he had been told that some Fenians had were seen there the previous night. He wondered what they could have been doing. He was upset that they had run the Carson family out of the area as Mrs. Carson had readily given them poitin and apple tart when they were on manoeuvres in her area. He missed her.

Having completed his inspection of the car he hurried into the house to give Olive a kiss before he left. She was making scones and her hands were covered in flour. She raised them high in the air before Albert threw his arms about her. She well knew the importance of keeping flour off the uniform. "I'm off, Olive" he said, letting her go, "I'll be late tonight".

"Goodbye, darling" she replied.

Albert sat into his car, turned on Downtown Radio, roared the 3-litre into life and left in a cloud of dust, racing towards Whitehall Cross. Olive went to the window and waved one floury hand after him. She stood there for a time looking down the hill. She admired the daffodils, Whitehall Bridge and the Silees River in the distance and considered that the ancestors who had built the house high up and well into the side of the hill were clever with their choice of situation. She had always loved the house – a Georgian two-storey over a tiny basement which contained the larder, and the dairy where the milk used to sit in big pans waiting for the cream to rise for churning into butter. The house had been

3

added to over the years so it was a bit spread about, but Olive believed that this added to its charm. The whole front of the house was covered in a purple-leaved grape vine. In good summers the grapes were edible and she thought about her daughters, Heather and Florence, leaning out of the bedroom windows to get the biggest and best bunches. Her daughters were much in her mind at that time. She hoped that Heather would do well in her 'O' levels. Her English and typing were good. There might be a chance of a job in Ormsbys. She knew that one of the girls in the office was pregnant and would be leaving soon. The Ormsbys were Albert's family solicitors and her own family had strong connections with them. (They were Protestants like the Elliots.) The pregnant girl's job could be Heather's even if her results were only average. And Olive had been good to Anna at one time, and look where she was now – senior partner in the firm. Wasn't she there when Anna's baby was born without the doubtful benefit of marriage, and it was Olive's own cousin who had adopted the child. Strange business, that – Anna having a relationship with a Fenian. Olive could never understand it.

Florence, on the other hand, could look after herself. She smiled with satisfaction as she thought of her aristocratic high forehead, fine grey eyes, wonderful colouring and the ash blonde hair, not to mention her slim, well-shaped body and endlessly long legs. Florence will get on just fine, she thought. She has a sweet nature. Her resemblance to her sister Thelma was disturbing at times but Olive kept putting it to the back of her mind. Florence had an innocence about her – not like Thelma, with her husky voice and earthiness.

4

Her reverie was suddenly forgotten. The house shuddered and the heavy mirror over the range fell down and shattered all over the kitchen floor. "ALBERT!" she cried out.

She stumbled as she fled towards the tractor in the yard. The key was in the ignition. She clambered up onto the seat, started the engine and tore off, bumping down the road past Key's entry, sweeping past Goodwin's Barn down the long hill through the chicane and there in front of her, through the smoke, the red Capri crumpled past all recognition – the big ash tree split in two – and the awful sweet smell of cordite. She thought her face would burst with the surge of blood that rushed there, but then it drained just as suddenly and she fainted.

* * *

The ambulance came out from Enniskillen and brought Olive to casualty in the Erne Hospital. Her forehead hurt. The nurse who looked after her was from Kesh – Sadie Bloomfield. One of themselves. She gave Olive fifty milligrams of Pethedene and two tablets of Librium. Please God that'll calm her for at least ten hours, Sadie said to herself.

* * *

When Olive woke she could hear that the house was full of people. She dressed with difficulty, forgot to brush her hair and wandered down to the kitchen. Her sister had arrived from Portglentoo. Everything was a mess. Albert's sisters were making sandwiches - egg and onion, ham and chicken, home-made brown bread and butter all scattered about. A helicopter, with its rotor turning slowly, stood on the large sweep of driveway in front of the house. Three aides-de-camp, all in full attire, were tucking into sandwiches and coffee. They stood up the minute she came into the room and strode towards her offering their sympathy. She was bewildered. She looked about for Albert. Albert's sister, Winifred, came towards her, all concern. "Ah Olive! Will you go a cup of coffee?" Olive took the cup mechanically. Winifred continued, "The Colonel wants to talk to you. He's waiting in the drawing room with your sister. And the Bishop says he will be here in half and hour."

Olive wished that they would all go away but she hadn't the strength to say anything. She remembered that Albert had never met Colonel Hyde-Whyte and supposed that the helicopter had something to do with his being there. Winifred then offered Olive two pills that the doctor had left for her and she obediently put them on her tongue and swallowed them with the coffee.

"Olive" said Winifred kindly, "come upstairs with me for a moment so you can brush your hair and put on a bit of make-up. You must put your best foot forward for your visitors."

Wearily Olive allowed all this, knowing that she really had no other option. "Winifred" she said, "I don't know what's happening to me but I'm glad you're here. You're always here when you're needed." Winifred smiled acknowledgement and then hugged Olive. Suddenly Olive began to cry. Albert was always about, but from now on there would be no Albert. Not today, not tomorrow, not ever. "Fuck!" she shouted, for the first time in her life. "Fuck the Fenians!" Winifred, being Winifred, said nothing.

Downstairs in the drawing room Olive met Colonel Hyde-Whyte, a tall, youthful, authoritative man who introduced himself and sympathised in a formal military way. Olive could not really concentrate on what he was saying because all she could think of was Albert. But he did say all sorts of kind things about her husband and his recent promotion and that he had served his Company, his Queen and his country with honour. When the formalities were over he introduced her to Major Henderson who said he wished to speak to her in private.

Olive had never really liked Major Henderson. She always felt there was something shifty about him. They went to the dining room, where they wouldn't be disturbed, and there he handed her a large brown envelope. He said there were five thousand pounds in it and that she should put it away safely. He also reassured her that the Regiment would take care of her. "Please don't worry" he said. How could she not worry with Albert gone! "Florence!" she called. Florence came immediately, her eyes red from crying. "What is it, Mum?"

"Please put this in the wardrobe in the big bedroom and then lock both it and the bedroom door and bring me the keys. I don't think I could make it up the stairs myself."

The Major continued, "I have a telegram from Her Majesty the Queen, and Prince Philip. I also have a telegram for you from Prince Charles and Princess Diana. Knowing the way

7

you feel, I doubt if you want to know about the one which came from McCaughey and the Free Staters. I put it in the bin anyway. The Royal Ulster Constabulary is convinced your husband was killed by Free Staters from Belduff. The Group will deal with them. However, the fact that a local lad has been seen by one of Captain Darcy's chappies drinking in O'Moore's in Belduff is much more sinister. He's from Donstown, Keown's his name. The RUC is anxious to get him to help them with their inquiries. Our local sleeper also reckons he did it."

The door opened, "Oh Olive, I know you said you were not to be disturbed, but some local has been stopped at the foot of the lane, says he's Patrick Maguire, has no ID and says he is the gravedigger" wailed the sister, who was no longer familiar with the area. "He says he must speak to you personally".

"He's harmless" said Olive listlessly.

"Harmless or not" responded the Major, "he must be searched thoroughly, as the place is coming down with VIPs. Check him for a handgun."

"Good God!" exploded Florence, who had just come back into the room and heard the end of the conversation, "it's Sharpening- stone! No one would give him a handgun. He might shoot himself! He only wants directions on where to dig the grave." She left and a couple of minutes later and returned with the gravedigger. Aged about forty-five, he was tall and dark-haired. While he wouldn't be considered good-looking, he had a certain air about him – as if he would be at ease in any company. He rushed over to where Olive sat and, grasping both her hands in his he said, "Jesus Christ, Olive, I am so sorry about Albert. He was a great friend of mine." But Olive wasn't listening. She was wondering where Thelma was and looked listlessly out of the window to see if her Jaguar was outside. She was also thinking that she must get rid of Sharpening-stone immediately, before Thelma arrived. She had always known that behind the pretence of not liking the man, Thelma harboured a longing for him. "Patrick" she said, as firmly as she could, "we will bury him in the family plot in the churchyard of St. Anne's in Kilmacowen. You know where the family plot is."

"I wish Thelma would come now," Olive said on an outgoing sigh. Patrick responded quickly, "She'll come just as soon as she can. She won't let you down," adding, "they are trigger happy. People will be taken out in retaliation. All hell's going to break loose, Olive," he paused, stared out the window, absentmindedly lit a cigarette and said, "Jesus, Olive" I don't know how I'll cope if I have to see Thelma again. You are the only one who knew how close we were. After she left I searched the dancehalls of Fermanagh, no, the whole of Ulster, looking for her."

"For God's sake, Patrick" said Olive wearily, "get a grip on yourself. I have told you a thousand times that she is happily married with grown-up children."

"I bet she's still beautiful," insisted Patrick. "Do you remember she was Lady of the Lake twenty-two years ago? She was the best-looking girl I ever clapped eyes on."

"Oh for God's sake Patrick, give it up will you! We have more to be thinking of. How much do you charge for a grave?"

"Ah now Olive," said Patrick, "I wouldn't charge you or Albert anything. I would consider it an honour to dig his grave. He was good to me."

"Patrick, how much do people normally give you?" Olive tried again.

"Twenty pounds" he said quickly, "but I wouldn't charge you."

"Heather," called Olive, "please bring me my handbag." She opened her purse and pushed a twenty-pound note down into his breast pocket. "Now," she said, "I must ask you to leave as I have the Bishop coming and he will want to speak to me on my own."

"Your Florence is very pretty," continued Patrick Maguire doggedly, "nearly as good-looking as her aunt. Tell Thelma when she comes that I spoke kindly about her."

I will in my eye tell her, thought Olive as she waved the gravedigger towards the door.

A huge Union Jack hung limply in the drizzle.

* * *

A large, long Ford came slowly up the avenue and parked in front of the house. The Bishop got out. He was new to the area and young, as Bishops go. He had established a good rapport with the people of his diocese for the short time he had been among them, and was known to be particularly good with the young people. Apart from the purple below the dog collar, one would not have guessed that he was a bishop at all. Olive welcomed him at the door. He silently took her hand in his. "Bishop," she said, in an obvious effort to have somebody make sense of the past number of hours, "tell me where God fits into this. Albert and I loved each other and he was an excellent father to the two girls. He attended church regularly, was a member of the Select Vestry, did all in his power to help his neighbours and lead a decent Christian life. I can think of nothing else but the sight of the car and the fact that my husband was in there somewhere, and there was absolutely nothing I could do for him." This all came out in a tearful rush while the Bishop listened sombrely and sympathetically.

Olive remembered her manners then and invited the Bishop inside. She introduced Winifred to him, who asked him if he would like a cup of tea. Having agreed to the tea, the Bishop sat down next to Olive. Taking her cold, shaking hand in his he said, "Let's just sit quietly for a moment and think about Albert being at peace now. I know that you will find this hard. It is a terrible time for you but please believe me when I say that I, and all your many friends, will do our best to help you and the girls through this." They sat for a time and then he said very quietly, "Shall we pray together?"

Pray! thought Olive incredulously. The last thing I want to do is pray! I don't think God was around when all this was happening to Albert. But once again her good manners prevailed and she bowed her head as the Bishop said the words that were meant to soothe and calm her. "Amen," she said and then, "So be it." But she did not accept it at all.

The Bishop drank his tea, which was by then very cold, and next asked to see Heather and Florence. Winifred went to fetch them.

* * *

The sleek black Jaguar crunched up the gravel and stopped in front of the house. The others in the room were startled when, with a strength they thought had left her, Olive shouted, "Thelma's here!" and got up and ran to the front door.

Out of the car got Thelma looking like a model from Jaeger's window in Donegal Square. At forty-four she oozed sex from every pore, and yet there was an air of discontent about her. The soldiers stood to attention long before her husband, the Assistant Commissioner of the RUC, got out of the car. They were mesmerised by her walk, her beauty. She was something else. "Olive!" she cried, "I am devastated! Poor Albert!" and then as she flung her arms around her sister she said more softly, "Poor you." Her voice was husky and intriguing, her perfume rich and expensive and Olive, for all her reservations about her sister, loved her and sobbed into her coat. They eventually went into the house together with Thelma's arm around Olive's shoulder.

"Now," said Thelma as they sat down "I don't want to be putting anyone to any bother and so we are staying at the Glebe House in Killadrone. I like the views of the lake from the bedroom windows there. I might as well indulge myself at the taxpayers expense. All the VIPs are staying there so security will be as tight as a duck's arse. Oh God, what a thing to have happened to Albert!"

Olive began to wonder why she had so wanted Thelma to come. She was suddenly irritated by her being there. She wanted peace so that she could think about Albert.

Another black car rounded Goodwin's Barn. Hammer-smiths, the undertakers, were coming with the body.

Major Henderson knocked on the door before coming in. He understandably thought that Thelma and Olive would not wish to be disturbed at a time when, as sisters, they needed each other most. He was surprised to find that Olive seemed relieved to see him. He said quietly, "Mrs. Elliot, the undertakers have arrived. Would you like me to have them put your husband in here?"

"Yes, thank you, Major" said Olive with her hand to her mouth, the true horror suddenly striking her. Thelma did not speak, just nodded. Major Henderson thought that this particular sister wasn't going to be much comfort here.

"Please allow me to look after all of this for you." He added, "Perhaps you should go and lie down for a little while?"

"No, please," said Olive. "I want to see Albert". The Major put his arm awkwardly around her shoulders and explained as best he could that the coffin would remain closed and that she would have to remember her husband as he was. Thelma still said nothing. Olive suddenly thought about her daughters and what they must be going through. "I'll go to the kitchen to the girls," she said, and quickly opened the door before they could stop her. She was confronted by Hammersmiths' men with the coffin. Sobbing, she rushed past them into the kitchen where she was comforted by her daughters and the women.

* * *

Winifred was greeting the Rector, Mr. Warrington, and his wife and her two sisters. The group of mourners parted to allow them access to Olive, and they murmured their condolences. Olive thanked them silently, her eyes raw from rubbing away the tears. As Mr. Warrington intimated that he wanted to speak to Olive on her own, the others backed away and left the two together.

Mr. Warrington wanted to know from Olive what hymns she thought Albert would have liked for his funeral service. As she seemed put out by his asking, he suggested kindly that perhaps he would have liked "The Lord's my Shepherd" and "Abide With Me".

"Ah Rector," said Olive sadly, finally focusing on the question she had been asked, "Albert would not have wanted those at all. He reckoned people were sad enough at funerals without choking their way through those hymns. I think

14

he would have liked, "Shall We Gather at the River". He liked hymns to be rousing, you know. He also loved "Onward Christian Soldiers". And I would like to have "For the Beauty of the Earth" because Albert loved nature and animals."

"Well, that's fine then," said Mr. Warrington. "I will tell the choir. You do realise, Olive, that the Bishop is preaching at the service? He has also asked the cathedral choir to come and join us, and the BBC and UTV are sending outside broadcast units."

Olive thought weakly about all of this pomp and ceremony and she felt tired and wished that it were all over and she could be left alone. Mr. Warrington then asked if there was anyone whom she would especially like to read the lesson. "No," said the widow firmly. "Please look after that for me, Rector. Where is Winifred?" Mr. Warrington took this last statement as his cue to go and, collecting his womenfolk, he left.

* * *

The telephone rang. "WHAT! I don't believe she's coming! Yes, we have enough men on the ground...maybe make the RUC aware on a need-to-know basis." Slamming the receiver down and with his face crumpled in panic, Major Henderson waved his hand agitatedly and roared, "Everybody stop talking! The Prime Minister had just left Northolt!" And then, gaining more control he said fairly calmly, "She will be here at 16.00 hours. She's fuming.

She wants Ken Beamish here when she arrives. Has anyone got Ken's number?"

There was pandemonium. Hoover, dishwasher, Brasso out for the two bronzes over the mantelpiece, the good Beleek Black Stamp antique china was taken from the cabinet and washed – it had been a wedding present from the Regiment. More brown bread, freshly baked by a neighbour was brought in, smoked salmon to replace the chicken and ham. God, how those women came into their own! It was as if they had been waiting for this signal to put them into overdrive. They had been waiting impatiently for something important to do, and this was it. Mrs. Whicker was on her way and they were part of it!

The helicopter arrived at exactly 16.00 hours. The women hid behind each other, wanting to see but not wanting to be seen. The uniformed men took over and respectfully showed the Prime Minister into the drawing room where she sympathised formally with Olive. Mrs. Whicker, fixing her handbag authoritatively on her forearm, checking that every hair was in place and that the left seam of the tweed skirt was straight, continued, "I am going to strengthen the security forces by moving in three hundred SAS men as soon as possible. You, Major, will deal with this by giving new instructions to the counter-terrorists. I am immediately going to instruct the Royal Engineers to build towers close to the frontier. These people must be stopped in their tracks, I say! They should be shot before they cross the Border, or even at the crossings themselves!" The watching women were held in thrall by her dominance. She added, "That's all, men! I will stand under the Union Jack for a photocall," and then more loudly she said again, "I will stand for photocalls under the Union Jack so hurry up, will you! I have to meet Chancellor Kohl at nine o'clock." The photographers did their duty hurriedly while she muttered under her breath, smiling through clenched teeth, "...and I will give him worse than I gave the Frogs last week!" Bowing slightly in Olive's direction, she left the house. Olive, in return, nodded in acceptance to her retreating back.

Major Henderson picked up the telephone receiver and dialled Captain Darcy's number. "I will meet you at 14.00 hours, Jamieson's office, Whitehall on Friday. Don't start the meeting without me. Goodbye!" As he was speaking, the chinooke blade turned slowly, and gradually the helicopter lifted up through the drizzle. The watchers could see Mrs. Whicker sitting by the window thumbing through files.

The day wore on with the people still coming to commiserate with the family. Last to arrive was Albert's brother Robert and his wife Daisy. Sadly, Olive recognised in him all that her husband had admired...his height at six foot two, his Inspector's uniform. It had been such a disappointment for Albert that he wasn't tall enough for the Force. He had been justifiably proud of his brother, but still, Albert was the best. With the thought came the awful realisation again that he was dead.

At eleven o'clock Winifred decided that the family had had enough and so she sent the mourners home and packed those who were staying in the house off to bed. Because the house was so full, Olive lay between her daughters in the large bed that had been her's and Albert's. "How will I cope with the loneliness?" she asked herself. "How will I cope with having no one to hold me and tell me he loves me? How will I manage to take all the family decisions on my own?" And so she sobbed throughout the night and finally, as the dawn light began to filter through the curtains, she fell asleep, exhausted.

* * *

Dear God! thought Patrick Maguire, but it never stops raining in this bloody country! In the summer Lough Erne is in Fermanagh. In winter Fermanagh is in the lake. He got into his ancient Datsun and had to slam the door twice before it shut to his liking. He pulled out of Monument Hill, the housing estate where he lived near the town of Enniskillen, and drove past the aerodrome. On the broad road in front of him he saw the Police and UDR patrol, so he reached to open the pocket on the dash of his car to take out his driving licence. The small UDR man signalled him to stop and ambled towards him.

"Where are you going?" he asked. Patrick replied that he was off to St. Anne's church in Kilmacowen to dig the grave for Albert Elliot. "Don't I know you from somewhere?" the little man asked and then added, remembering, "You're from Monument Hill, aren't you?"

"I am indeed," replied the gravedigger, "lived there for a good while now. You know," he said confidentially, I fancied Albert Elliot's sister-in-law but she preferred and married one of your own top buck cats."

The little man was obviously not much impressed by this bit of information and said, "That was a bad do with that poor man."

"Well indeed it was," said Patrick. "He was one of the best – a good friend of mine, you know, and a good farmer into the bargain. Well, I'd best be getting on with my job. It's a rotten day for digging a grave. The clay in yon graveyard is blue daub and it's wet and there's no shelter up on that hill. But sure, there's no use in complaining.

"Well there's not," said the UDR man. "Mind the security now and drive carefully." He waved Patrick on and signalled the next car to stop.

Patrick pulled up at the church gate beside lots of other cars and Outside Broadcast Units. Putting on his old working anorak, he went to the boot and took out his spade, pickaxe and shovel. He looked at the sky and noted that the wind was moving the clouds along nicely, and that the weather was clearing from Beleek. Shouldering his tools, he went through the open gate and was glad to see that the men who had offered to gather the moss to line the grave had been as good as their word and had left plenty of it inside behind the pillar for him. He took pride in making his graves look as good as possible. He took no notice of the activity of the members of the Mothers' Union who went in and out of the church with fresh flowers and dusters and polish, all the while murmuring in lowered voices. He took no notice either of the television crews that were setting up. He had his own job to get on with.

He set to work and removed his anorak after about ten minutes when the rain reduced to a light drizzle. He worked on steadily until the grave had been dug and lined. He climbed out and, hearing his stomach rumble, he gathered his gear and went back to the car for his flask and sandwiches. With the car door open, he sat sideways in the driver's seat with his feet on the ground, and poured himself a cup of tea. Munching his sandwiches he viewed the surrounding countryside from his vantage point on the top of the hill. A weak sun filtered hesitatingly through the broken cloud and Patrick thought that perhaps it would not rain on Albert's funeral after all. Tidying up the remains of his lunch, he swung his legs into the car, slammed the door twice out of habit, and went back to Monument Hill to change his clothes. He had to get back to the church for three o'clock when the funeral was due to take place.

* * *

Thelma pranced into the drawing room where Olive sat, on her own, staring into the fire, and closed the door behind her. It was the morning of the funeral. Getting right to the point Thelma said, "Do you ever see Sharpening Stone?"

Olive was shocked into saying, "Thelma! That was an awful name you called the poor man and I always feel ashamed for you that it stuck."

"Ah yes…" said Thelma excitedly, bursting to continue. Olive stopped her flow by saying, "Anyway, if I had seen him I wouldn't tell you, but I'll let you know this much – he is digging the grave at the moment. She was shocked at the white lie she had just told but reckoned she was justified under the circumstances.

Thelma filled the pause by continuing, "Do you remember the night Albert and you and I went to the dance in Fivemiletown?"

"I do," said Olive evenly.

"Well," said Thelma, if you remember, I went outside before you and Albert did, and he was there waiting for me. That was the night I saw his dick and I swear to God it was just like Mother's sharpening stone. It was every bit as hard and much the same shape. I thought he was going to kill me with it! When I offered him a condom, he told me those things were a mortal sin and he didn't believe in protection, but in procreation. I am as sure as anything that if I'd stayed in this neck of the woods I would have finished up in the pudding club with six or seven children, eking out an existence in Kilmacormack. Am I thankful that instead I have my huge house overlooking Bangor Bay and all that goes with my husband's job – and money! Thanks a lot, Sharpening- stone, but no thanks!"

"Will she ever shut up!" thought Olive. "My husband's been blown to pieces, my life is in ruins and all my sister can talk about is lust and sex, that I will never have again." Looking at Olive, Thelma realised that she had gone too far, but secretly she was wondering what an affair with Sharpening-stone would be like. Her husband had class and money but she was bored to death with him. She'd had affairs with men in the Force but they never amounted to much – just the odd bit of sex snatched here and there and saying things she didn't mean and writhing and getting no satisfaction.

She left Olive staring into the fire again.

* * *

Patrick got back to the church in plenty of time and took up a good position by the outside of the churchyard wall. He had had a word with the security men and they let him be. He watched the funeral cortege make its way slowly up the steep hill and suddenly felt very sad. Painfully slowly, the mourners and dignitaries filled the little church to capacity, while the overflow stood silently outside in the weak sunshine as the service began.

Patrick, with head bowed a little, and looking out from under his eyebrows, had respectfully watched the first few members of the mourning family file past him – and then he saw Thelma. "Jesus Christ!" he hissed through clenched teeth. For him she had not aged one whit and on him, even after twenty odd years, she still had the same electrifying effect. He felt weak and strong all at once and the feeling excited him to an embarrassing degree. Thanks be to God, he said to himself, we are all faced the same way! His eyes followed her and, with that, she spotted him and for one split second their eyes met and he detected, on her beautiful face, the slightest blush. He was angry with his eyes then because they filled with miniscule tears, and the vision that he had conjured and re-conjured for all those years and which was now there in reality became blurred. And by the time he had swiftly wiped his eyes clear again, she had moved on and become lost in the throng.

There was mayhem in Patrick Maguire's head and heart. He upset himself by remembering, thrust by thrust, the time they had made incredible love in Will's meadow, behind the Protestant dance hall, with the noise of the corncrakes mixing poorly with the sound of that bloody awful dance band. And he remembered, as if it were five minutes ago, that the band was making a desperate job of "Save the Last Dance for Me" when Thelma agreed to lie down, and that it was going to be followed by "God Save the Queen", and if the love-making didn't finish soon they would be caught by the Protestant courting couples who always used Will's field after a Parish Social – with no thought whatsoever for the crop of hay that was due to be cut. Then he bothered himself with wondering if he had really seen her blush, and if she was blushing, whether or not it was because she too remembered the field.

Patrick Maguire heard no hymns sung by the grouped choirs, no readings from the Bible, no address by the Bishop, no Nunc Dimittis, nothing – even though the whole service was relayed to the silent people outside by loudspeakers. Suddenly he realised that the coffin was being carried towards the open grave, preceded by the Rector, and that Dick Winters, his rugby idol and a member of the Republic's government, was walking towards the grave also. "If I get a chance at all," he thought, "I must shake that fellow by the hand." He felt someone touch his shoulder and it was Hammersmith, the undertaker. He pushed a twenty-pound note into Patrick's breast pocket and said, "Thanks Pat. You did a good job."

"It was a pleasure," responded Patrick, and was about to say what good friends he and Albert had been, but got no chance because Hammersmith moved on.

No sooner had Hammersmith left than Robert, Albert's brother, sought him out. "I understand," he said, "that you dug Albert's grave this morning?"

"Well, I did," said Patrick, "but then Albert was a good friend..."

"Anyway," said Robert interrupting, "here's a little money for you and thank you" and he pushed a twenty-pound note into the gravedigger's hand. The crowd was beginning to disperse quickly because the rain, which had held off so valiantly for the funeral, began to fall again and the sky was darkening with the promise of more and heavier rain to follow. Patrick went to the car for his oilskins, Wellingtons and shovel. He had to fill the grave once the graveyard was empty, and he wanted to get it done fast. He had been invited to the local hotel for some food and drink – as had all those who had helped with the funeral – and the thought especially appealed to him at that moment. As he turned, Thelma swept by, leaving with him the heady smell of her Chanel No 5 and the swirl of her mink coat. And this time, he thought, there was no blush and no recognition, so I've made it all up – the way I sometimes feel I've made up everything about her. And with a sinking feeling he made his way to the pile of earth and began to shovel.

The rhythm soothed him and he worked away and never noticed the rain which seeped through the old oilskins. Hammersmith Junior, the undertaker's son, stood for a moment to watch. "Pat," he said, "you did a fine job, so I'll give you ten pounds over the normal," and he pushed two crisp notes into the waiting hand. "Jesus!' thought Patrick, "this is mighty! Seventy quid in a day!"

Every so often he would stop and rest and watch the television crew clearing up their stuff and finally the Church Warden locked the church and shouted goodbye. He worked on and did not notice the car drive up. He didn't even turn when he heard the footsteps because he was straining to get his job finished.

Two warm hands suddenly covered his eyes and to his nostrils came the scent of the Chanel No 5. "Guess who?" said Thelma brightly.

Patrick let his shovel fall on the almost-level grave and removed the incredible blindfold slowly. Slowly he turned to face her. Not one word was said as he carefully placed his wet, dirty, callused hands on either side of the adored face – and then he closed his eyes and kissed her with the rain falling all around. Never, never had Thelma been kissed like this before, and through the mink and the oilskins she could feel his erection grow and she was thrilled and passionate and yearned for him.

When he opened his eyes to look at her she said urgently, and with a seriousness that he did not expect, "I'm coming to see you on Monday – at your house. Is that alright? Will you give me your telephone number?"

"Sure, it's in the book, Thelma," he said quietly.

"Of course," she said, "I'm so used to everyone being ex-directory. I'll phone you on Sunday night about nine to arrange a time." And reaching up to brush her lips against his, she turned and left him standing on the top of the hill in the graveyard, his hands hanging loosely by his sides and with the night settling in.

II

Captain Darcy drove to Portglentoo. He was cruising along steadily and came to the sign that said he was welcome to the town. Alongside this was the graffiti that quipped, amongst other things, "F.T.P" (Fuck the Pope) and "Shoot them all! Let God sort them out!" That says everything, he thought, I'm classed, for my Catholicism, as one of those. This little area is both the armpit and the anvil of Northern Ireland. This will be the last place of horror before these Troubles wear themselves out.

He pulled in at the first car sales establishment he came to. A dapper little salesman came forward and Darcy asked him if he could see his boss. "Which one of the bosses would you like?" enquired the man.

"Either of them will do," said Darcy matter-of-factly. "Just say that Captain Darcy is here." He sat back into his car to wait and looked at the vehicles gleaming all around him. Alexander came out of his office at the back of the building and greeted Darcy warmly. "Damp old day, isn't it?" he asked, and was about to launch into more about the weather but changed his tack to ask, "Can I sell you a car?"

"No," said Darcy quickly, but you could leave the keys in that big black 3-litre Ford Granada when you finish tomorrow evening." Alexander got the gist immediately. "Leave them under the carpet on the driver's side."

"OK," replied the garage owner, "but I'll need a certificate."

"That's not a problem. The Assistant Chief can look after that. He's due at the meeting tonight," said Darcy getting back into his car. He rolled down the window and said, "Where's the Chairman, by the way?"

"Him!" snorted Alexander. "He's always at the Bank!"

"I need to talk to Billy and Robin. It's about that nasty incident in Fermanagh."

"Ah" sighed Alexander nodding, "You will only need to see the Chairman and the two lads at the moment."

"Yes, I know," said Darcy curtly, "just buzz the three of them for me and tell them I will meet them in fifteen minutes in the Dolphin Bar." He closed the window to stop the rain spitting in on him and drove out into the road.

The Dolphin Bar was a dingy spot with tartan carpets that badly needed cleaning and dark brown paint everywhere – a depressing place at the best of times, but even worse at eleven o'clock in the morning. The smell of stale cigarette smoke was sickening. Darcy ordered a gin and tonic with ice and lemon, was out of luck with the ice, and looked at the pictures of the racehorses that were hung all over the walls – along with one of the Queen, framed in royal blue.

There was also a worthy record in tapestry of the names and dates of the battles fought by the Royal Inniskilling Fuisileers.

He did not have long to wait before the Chairman came in. He was without the lads because, as he explained apologetically to Darcy, they were still in bed, but he had told them to get up and they would be along soon. He was glad, he said, that Captain Darcy was in town because he always got the right terrorist. The Captain smiled wanly. "Fellows like you," the Chairman continued with gusto, "can bring Ulster back from the abyss!" With that the door from the street opened and the two men turned to meet the notorious Jackal and King Rat.

"Hello Robin, Hello Billy," Darcy said without much enthusiasm. "It's been a while since we've met. I don't think we've seen each other since those little affairs in Monaghan and Dublin." The men agreed. "I heard you got Sam Marshall, the bastard, and you did well to get Tommy Casey too." He did not elaborate further. He was not a man for platitudes and never wasted time in speaking to these two men whom he particularly detested. He knew they were cruel in the extreme, and he resented the fact that they were instrumental to his plans. "I wanted to see you to confirm arrangements for a strike on the two terrorists in Belduff – the ones who were implicated in the assassination of that UDR man in Fermanagh. His brother-in-law is very friendly with the Chairman here. He's a customer of his bank and a potential new member of our Group. He is due to be appointed Assistant Chief Constable. He will automatically be an ex-officio member of the Group – able to attend meetings but not entitled to vote. I will give you five hundred pounds each when I am happy that the car you will use has been burned."

The Chairman interrupted, "The strike must be ratified by the full Group, but I don't think there will be any dissenting voice or voices. The Chaplain even wants to go on active service on the strike! We will use him later." The men listened, smiling and nodding. They understood perfectly.

"I want those bastards finished off," said Darcy. He explained the rest of the details and added, "The car will not be reported missing until it has been dumped and burned – something to do with a Chief Constable certificate. And no drinking on the job! I will meet you at Kilboo Cross. I have marked it on this map for you in red biro. It is on the Belduff/Garridon road. Tonight I will go to London for the money and the sanction for the weaponry. Goodbye and thankyou, Chairman! Please give my regards to Thelma when next you meet her."

"Actually, I will be dining with her and her husband next Wednesday night, come to think of it," said the Chairman.

"Don't forget now!" said Darcy turning to address the two men for further emphasis. "22.00 hours, and NO drinking!" This time he took full stock of the Jackal, realising for the first time how shrunken and emaciated he looked. The cancer he had been told about was taking hold.

* * *

On the dot of 20.00 hours, Captain Darcy strode into the foyer of the Oceango Hotel. At the reception desk he was told which room had been assigned for the meeting and immediately went there. He knocked on the door and it was opened for him by the Chairman of the Group. Smiling politely Darcy said, "We seem to meet rather a lot these days!" The Chairman nodded and showed him into the room. He looked around at those gathered and was surprised to see amongst them the Reverend Shane Glasgow. He took his allotted seat at the table and the meeting was immediately called to order. The bank-managing Chairman called on the Chaplain to open the meeting with prayer. The grey-suited man asked all present to stand and bow their heads. He fervently prayed, "Direct us, O Lord, in all our deliberations this evening. Give us wisdom and strength to carry out Your will. Help us to make wise judgements and decisions and grant us courage to carry them out. Through Jesus Christ Our Lord, Amen."

"Amen," chorused the gathering earnestly before sitting down to begin the business of the meeting.

Before the minutes of the previous meeting were read and adopted, the Chairman welcomed the Reverend Shane Glasgow and Captain Darcy. Having got no further than explaining that his Reverence was a staunch man in the defence of Ulster, Shane Glasgow leapt to his feet and launched into a type of speech to which those present were well used. They had read similar words in accounts of his rallies in the newspapers, and had witnessed the same vitriolic verbosity from him on their television screens.

"Gentlemen," he began, "we are surrounded by demons! Washington, the European Union, The Papacy and the British and Irish Governments are all hell-bent on dragging Ulster into Perdition! Fascism and the Child of Rome are alive and well! There is no lie too black, no crime too washed in crimson blood, no murder too Satanic, no bank robbery too monstrous but the IRA will be in there achieving its hellish ends." He looked around at the seated men and was content to note that they were all, with the exception of Darcy, listening earnestly and in agreement with him.

So, further motivated, he went on. "They have been brainwashed by the Jesuits!" he said, his voice rising. "Neither the cries of the orphans nor the agony of widows upset them! Their activities are neither curbed by the sorrows of the bereaved nor the outrage of the people! They enjoy wading knee-deep in Protestant blood! They delight in killing!"

By this stage Glasgow could sense that the Chairman was about to stop him in his tracks so he quickly continued, "The Mass is a blasphemy and it's in the Roman Catholic Churches that this blasphemy is celebrated! The SAS must be recalled! Strengthened rings of steel must be thrown around the Roman Catholic ghettos! Internment must be re-introduced!" Knowing his time had run out he shouted, "We must overcome the heathens among us!" and sat down.

In the silence that followed the Chairman quietly pointed his finger at Glasgow, looked at him squarely and said, "There will be a bullet put in you if you make any arrangements with Dublin." The Reverend was gobsmacked.

The business of the meeting got underway.

The ritualistic burning of some churches before the twelfth of July was decided upon, as was the number of coach loads of Orangemen who would be brought to Dunree, on the actual day, for the church service – twenty from Antrim, fifteen from Lisburn, twelve from Ballymena, eight from Enniskillen and five from Omagh. They were exhorted to dress well and to bring the odd paling post in case any Pope Heads needed a bashing. The march down the Sarne Road took a lot of consideration and it was decided to tell the supporters to prepare for a long haul in case the residents became unmannerly.

Captain Darcy's reason for being at the meeting was evident when the question of two murderers who needed to be eliminated came up. His plan had been circulated to each member of the Group and it was unanimously agreed upon. He was thanked for jobs well done in Monaghan and Dublin.

Next to be considered was the concern expressed by Loyalists over the increasing numbers of Roman Catholics who were moving to live among them in Portglentoo. The Chairman said that up to now it had been a Taig-free zone and that it was the Group's intention to keep it that way. It was agreed that a petrol bomb or two should be used to show this vermin that it was not welcome. The meeting unanimously decided that the best time to carry out this agenda would be after the Twelfth when the Reverend Shane Glasgow had stirred things up a little.

"I could easily muster a group of youngsters then," said a professor, another member of the Group. "They would be delighted to do as I said!" The Chairman pointed out, unnecessarily, that if this wasn't done they could be faced with another Sarne Road situation in the near future. "Swift action," he said, "would bring swift results." He thanked the professor on behalf of the Group for his co-operation.

There was no further business and so the Chaplain ended the meeting with prayer.

As the members gathered up their notes and prepared to leave, Captain Darcy sidled up to the professor and asked him for help with a new programme he was setting up. All that would be needed was for the Captain to bring himself and a ream of paper with him to Queen's University. The professor gave him directions to his rooms and then they parted company.

* * *

"Department of the Navy," it read on the giant doors looking out on Whitehall five stories up. "Graham Jamieson."

Jamieson paced up and down his office nervously. Apart from his worried look there was nothing about him that stood out particularly. He was a little portly, was small and wore the regulation grey suit. He was forty-seven but looked older and his hair was thinning. Because he was sweating he decided that the next day he would ask to have the heating in his office turned down a little. He had previously worked in the Pensions section, but after the Falklands War he was moved to Counter-Terrorism. His detail was to lose his budget in the Defence Department and to pay monies and wages. This one was easy. No budget had been sanctioned by Charles Kingston and countersigned by the Cabinet Secretary. It was all his, and he was looking forward to it is a distraught sort of way. He distractedly thought about his mother and her steadily increasing nursing home bills. She was dying of cancer and he owed a great deal of money for her care.

Mr. Jamieson was waiting for Captain Darcy and Major Henderson. He considered that Darcy was getting out of control. He'd got a bit of a land himself when he was summoned to the Home Office by the Minister for Home Affairs. He'd got one hell of a ticking off because Darcy had put the bombs in Monaghan and Dublin. All of Whitehall was aghast and the legal and political implications were horrendous.

There was a sharp knock on his door, and without waiting for any word to indicate that it was convenient to go in, Captain Darcy arrived. "Good evening Captain!" said Jamieson a little startled. "How have you been since we last met?" While they spoke Jamieson was thinking how Darcy had aged and become gaunt. Sleeping rough was obviously taking its toll and a transfer would be the best thing from him. But Darcy would not be transferred because he was good, in fact he was probably the best counter-terrorist in the business. He explained that he had had a phone call from Major Henderson who would join them in the next five minutes and then he asked, "Would you like a drink?" He handed the Captain a glass and then poured him a Johnny Walker, afterwards pouring a large one for himself. Without bothering to ask whether or not Jamieson objected to smoking in his office, Darcy lit a cheroot and blew the smoke nonchalantly towards the ceiling.

"Do sit down," said Jamieson, pointing to the chair on the far side of his desk. "I want to take you though some details." Looking thoughtfully at Darcy he murmured, "First we must discuss the laundry business…the one you have set up on the Highgate Road. I have no real problems with it, as the information and surveillance have both been excellent. It has identified most of the subversives in the Highgate area. I have been looking through your files and I notice that you were educated at Ampleforth. The monks there would have difficulty with your second detail, which sits very uncomfortably in your file. Now…your whorehouse on the Causeway Road…the members of the WRAC are quite disconcerted and wish you to improve on pay structures. These women are not content with Army rates of pay but are prepared to negotiate better terms. I certainly no longer intend to fund it under its present format. I'm happy with the information it gives me, but I'm not keen on the set-up, to be honest. However, if you can renegotiate with the WRAC to its satisfaction then I will be prepared to continue with the funding."

Shifting in his chair, putting on his cross face and mustering all his courage Jamieson sat forward, stared into Darcy's face and thundered, "Who gave you permission to bomb

Monaghan and Dublin? You have put my job in jeopardy and consequently my pension is at risk. You've threatened the issuance of our funds. Whitehall has leapt all over me. Senior Civil Servants have been coming in and out of this office and tearing strips off me. I have told lies on your behalf. If you do this again," he said icily, "we will be had up in the International Court of Justice in the Hague, because if the Irish Government gets one whiff of what our section has been doing in the name of counter-terrorism, they will pass the responsibility back to Whitehall and we'd be cleaned out by the claims-conscious victims and their relatives."

Jamieson sat back and glared at Darcy.

"Mr. Jamieson, Sir!" answered Darcy patronisingly, "I have been at the coal face now for twelve years. While I appreciate your continual funding for the whorehouse and the launderette, I want to tell you that when I was put into counter-terrorism there were no limitations to my brief." He tapped the ash off the end of his cheroot and drew deeply on it again. Getting to his feet and filling the room with all of his six feet four inches he said, "Sometimes, when you have no limit you can make mistakes. Unfortunately, I may have been dragged on into the bombings by some subversives in our Section. In retrospect, I can see that counter-terrorism means the assassination of PIRA men without the necessity of bringing them through the courts. At the same time I will not apologise for what happened in Monaghan and Dublin because it's not possible to completely control the demons that violence release. Furthermore, I want to talk to you about the sleepers. These men have been at this job a long time and, as two of them are approaching their mid-forties, they wish to be considered for safer jobs. I want you to see to it that

Lieutenant Dickson is put in charge of security at the British Embassy in Washington with promotion to Captain. Ditto for Lieutenant Davidson in Paris."

Major Henderson marched into the room in much the same fashion as Darcy had done earlier. He accepted the shot of Johnny Walker and immediately Darcy began to speak as if absolutely nothing had passed between himself and Jamieson. "You first! I want ten-thousand pounds up front," he said, and then to Major Henderson, "the Group is looking after the car. Everything will be in order. The car will not be reported stolen until after it has been destroyed. The inner circle of the RUC will make sure there is no security on the roads we are using…the clearance for weapons and bullets is being drawn up down at Thiepval and the guns will not be returned. We need ammunition clips so arrange for me to collect them with registration plates, two handguns and four smoke grenades. Keown and O'Hare did the job on Albert Elliot. They were watched leaving their caravan at 05.00 hours with wires and paraphernalia. You see, O'Hare has the know-how and Keown knows the location. Keown's car had fifty-one miles up, which was just right and he got back about forty-five minutes after the incident. They each have five hundred punts in their pockets so they have got to be hit in the next ten days for us to succeed. You see, they may leave the area after that. We know that O'Hare's knowledge of explosives, command wires and semtex is such that he will be moved to another active service unit fairly soon."

Major Henderson thanked the Captain and said, "You can pick up your money and arms tomorrow." Looking at Jamieson he said,

"The car will be a black 3-litre Ford Granada. Please phone stores at Thiepval with the engine and chassis number. I can sanction all of this without referral."

He then asked Darcy what he thought about the murder of Albert Elliot and was told, "Well, this goes back a long way, but I will short-circuit it by saying that it is policy from the man in Clonniff to denude the Border of Loyalists, and, in taking out Albert Elliot, they have pushed the line a little bit further back. We are in retreat in all the border areas while he sits pretty in Clonniff. Tactically the Group is mad for action and I can't blame them. We must strike soon. I can guarantee three hit men from Portglentoo. I will arrange for the men to liase with the Captain at Kilboo Cross. I gather that these two drink every night in the Lounge of O'Moore's. If the Captain's man will identify them, the lads will solve the problem. They can meet you outside the Criterion at 10.30 hours if this is OK?"

Jamieson was thrilled that business was over for the day. The two men frightened the hell out of him but he was afraid to admit it – even to himself. He did his best to smile as they threw their whiskies straight down. "I look forward to seeing you again," he said to the retreating backs of the two military men. He didn't notice whether or not they replied.

* * *

In Thiepval Barracks in Lisburn things were calm when Captain Darcy walked in. Everything was ready for him in a corner of the ordnance room. He checked the contents, agreed that everything was in order, signed both the A65 and the A95 and, feeling that he couldn't get out of there fast enough, took his departure. Being part of the dirty tricks brigade had its disadvantages, he thought, and the sooner I am back on my own ground the better.

* * *

Captain Darcy stood at Kilboo Cross chewing a stalk of grass that he had picked out of the ditch, and looked down on Lough Melton. He had reached a milestone in his life and, while at one stage he had thrived in his chosen career, he was now beginning to wonder just what he was doing in this violent little country. He also wondered if he really belonged anywhere. He was so deep in thought that he was startled when a big, black Ford Granada spun up behind him and stopped. A large man with close-cut hair and an incredible stink of alcohol jumped out. It was King Rat.

"Hello Billy," he said evenly, "I've got stuff for you. No need to tell you how to use the weapons. There's five hundred for each of you, as arranged. The plan is that you put two bullets into Keown and two into O'Hare. No other killings, mind! That's very important. If the Southern Police find two known subversives dead, while they may not be happy, they won't go to the funerals." He sighed. Billy wasn't listening. No one listens. That's part of it. "Let's get on with it then," he said, shrugging his shoulders tiredly.

* * *

Thomas O'Donnell was in good voice in O'Moore's bar. He threw back his head and sang,

40

No more will he hear the seagulls cry
Over the river Shannon tide
For he fell beneath the northern skies
Brave Hanlon by his side.
He is gone to join that gallant band
Of Plunket, Pearse and Tone

Another martyr for Old Ireland
Sean South of Garryowen.

"Good on you, Tom!" shouted Keown. "Give us another song!"

Tom replied, "No fault of the company now, but I've got to go. I'm drunk out!" As there were plenty more to take his place on the podium, the gathering allowed him to leave. Pulling his duffel coat tightly around him, he left the bar just as the next entertainer began:

In Mountjoy Jail one Monday morning,
High upon the Gallows Tree,
Kevin Barry gave his young life
For the cause of Liberty.

Once out onto the footpath, Tom changed gait and sped to the waiting black Granada that was parked on the opposite side of the street down towards the bridge. "No time for talk, Tom," snapped Darcy. "Give the descriptions."

"OK," said Tom, speaking rapidly, "Back of the lounge. Keown in green gansey and blue jeans. Red hair. O'Hare's next him. Blue gansey, white polo neck."

"Got that, Billy?" asked Darcy. "Get on with it then."

As King Rat and Jackal left the car Tom pleaded to Darcy, "Captain, I can't stay here much longer."

"I know, I know Tom," said Darcy. "Don't worry. I have spoken to Jamieson. I will arrange a transfer for you. How do you feel about Washington?"

"I would go anywhere."

"I know Tom, God I do know!" said Darcy.

As Tom left the Granada he heard the shots and disappeared into the night. He could imagine the panic in the pub and the smoke from the grenades, the screaming women and the yelling children and, most horribly of all, he could visualise the smile on the Rat's face as he did the job he loved so well. He hoped that he would get away before they caught up with him. He tried not to think about it. It was better not to think about it.

* * *

"OK Billy?" asked Captain Darcy as the Granada spewed around the corner heading for Kinhest.

"Dead as last year's snow!" replied the man proudly. 'There's blood spilling out of both their heads. Dear God, but I did get great pleasure out of that!" He smiled, settling into his seat, confident that he had done the job well.

"Head for Inver," said Darcy to the driver. "I know a turn up a lane that'll take us to Kilboo Cross. After you leave me off, take the car to Barronscourt Forest. Phone Portglentoo for a lift home. After your lift arrives, put the original registration back on the car and then burn it. Report to me at Thiepval on Tuesday at 12.00 hours. In my office, there is five hundred for each of you, as I already said. I myself will personally deal with any deviation from the plan. Take these written instructions and do what they say. Go home now. Lie low. I'll be back in Portglentoo after I've made sure you've done what you were told. And, furthermore, I want to say that I think you are a shower of bastards! How do you expect to win this war when you arrive to do a job stinking of alcohol? Let me off here," he said with obvious disgust, "I am fed up with you gang of fools!" When the car stopped, he got out and slammed the door behind him.

* * *

When Jamieson picked up his Tuesday Telegraph, he was not surprised to read of the murder of two subversives in Belduff. It listed the incident as part of a number of tit-for-tat assassinations, blaming it on Loyalists from Portglentoo – someone called King Rat together with his colleagues. It sounded ominous, but there was no satisfaction for him knowing that he had funded the escapade. He knew that he would not sleep easy that night. He made up his mind to consider his position soon – but he wanted to get over the Easter Bank Holiday first.

III

M onday finally arrived. Patrick had spent the previous few days in his house painting. He had even tiled the bathroom – a job that had been waiting to be done for the longest time. The tiles were black and shiny and he hoped that they would impress Thelma. Then he began to worry that the smell of paint would give her a headache. He had one himself, brought on by the nervous anticipation he felt. He'd waited twenty years to see her and now that she was about to arrive into his life again – and in a manner so totally undreamed of – he felt ill. He looked at himself in the mirror and the face that looked back at him was pale. He combed his black wavy hair for the fourth time, checked that his breath was pure, decided that it wasn't and brushed his teeth again. He wiped his mouth with the towel and put it back neatly on the towel rail.

Looking out of the window he saw a taxi pull up at his gate and watched Thelma get out and pay the driver. He took a few deep breaths and went unsteadily down the stairs to open the door to his beloved.

"Welcome to Number 12" he said awkwardly. He knew it was a silly thing to say but it came out foolishly from his mouth and he wanted to kick himself for it. He took her hand, led her inside and closed the door. He would have loved for her to have thrown her arms around him and he was waiting, hoping that she would do so – but she didn't. As she marched in she was talking. Thelma always had so much to say. And she spoke so fast! He remembered this from before and he began to enjoy just listening to her.

"I've told that guy to come back for me in two hours. Here, where would you like me to put my things down?" she asked, shedding her coat and flinging it together with her large handbag onto the hall chair. "Make me a cup of tea like a good fellow! The traffic was dreadful on the way down. I had a horrid journey. I've left the car at The Kill-moylan. I dodged the heavies by taking a taxi. I have my own methods that would take too long to explain. They're not half so cute as they think, those boyos!" She stopped for a moment to look around her and then continued, "The house is quaint. I like it!" Patrick began to feel quite comfortable within himself. As long as the house had Thelma's approval he was happy. He made the tea and the two of them sat at the little table in the kitchen and he watched her intently while she drank. Hasn't she the lovely hands! he mused. And I love the way she raises that cup to her lips and I love the animated way she talks.

They discussed Albert's funeral and how Olive was coping and then the tea was finished and Thelma stood up and said matter-of-factly, "Let's go to bed."

She walked around the table and took Patrick by the hand. He got smartly to his feet and went before her up the stairs. He let go of her hand and went to draw the curtains. When he turned around it was to see the beauty of Thelma's naked body stepping out of the pool of clothes that she had hurriedly dropped around her slim ankles in the few seconds that his back was turned. He grasped her and hugged her to him kissing her passionately. She ducked out of his embrace finally and leapt into his bed, pulling the duvet around her and giggling. "Get your clothes off and come here you old goat!" she said. Patrick did not need to be asked. He plunged under the duvet beside her leaving a trail of clothes behind him.

She ran her hands over him and was thrilled by the length of him and the strength of him and the firmness of his body. She moved her exquisite frame, writhing over him, caressing her clitoris with his penis. He stroked the length of her back with the tips of his fingers and then, as she raised her body above his, he cupped her magnificent pendulous breasts in his huge hands. She yearned for him as he did for her and, in an instant, she steered his enormous size inside of her and gasped in agony because he had plumbed her depth to the utmost. Their bodies were unified in violent and rhythmic passion. As she climaxed for the first time she screamed and then she whispered savagely over and over again, "You do love me!" and he answered with more feeling than she had ever heard from any man, "Yes Thelma, I adore you! You are my beautiful, beautiful spearbhean!"

They rolled over as one and she knotted her legs around his and he thrust and thrust deeply, faster and faster until they came, together. Patrick very gently rolled off her and they lay quietly, side by side, he with his eyes closed, and he stroked her and she lay still.

Suddenly she said, staring at the ceiling, "And what do you see in that scrubber from Sligo that you visit every Friday night?"

Patrick's eyes shot open. "What scrubber?"

"Don't talk so far back!" she said, sitting up and looking at him. "She's on my husband's computer list. And I tell you, that one you see in Donegal town isn't a whole heap better! She's real low life! Did you know that she had a baby by a nigger?" Finished with that revelation, Thelma snuggled up to Patrick, trying to knot her long fingers in the silky hairs of his chest. She then moved her right thigh between his legs right up to his genitals and they eventually made love again. This time it was less urgent and more relaxed but still exquisite. She sat up lazily and looked at her man with the duvet falling away from her breasts and said, "Those two I mentioned before, they're dead from now on in. I won't tolerate your seeing anyone else."

I promise you I won't see either of them again my darling" he said, and she believed him and was content.

They dressed and went downstairs. She looked at her watch. "Would you like a drink before you go?" he asked. She nodded and he poured her a large Hennessy.

She tossed it back and said, "Next time, make that a Martell Gold Label please!" When Patrick looked perplexed she snorted, "And don't give me that poor mouth bit! I know all about your account in the bank in Cavan. The Chairman of the Group is a Director of that particular banking set-up.

He told me that you had seventy thousand pounds in a high yield investment. Where did you get it from?"

Patrick answered steadily, "I spent five years in New York working for an old uncle of mine. When he died he left me the bulk of his estate and, as you can see, I haven't much need of it. I lodged it in Cavan because I don't want the revenue to know about it and get cross with me."

"There's something else too" she went on. "I like fresh oysters. There is a man in Kildalkey who sells the best in this part of the world. As I'll be calling here most Mondays, pick up a dozen every Friday and put them in the freezer. If you take them out three hours before I get here, they'll be fine." She began to put her coat on.

"Thelma" said Patrick, "Can I ask you something?"

"Fire away" she said.

"Don't you like foreplay?"

"No" she answered with amusement, "Foreplay is for wimps. I like it just as it was today. And by the way," she said, changing the subject as if it was of no consequence, "whatever became of your brother the priest?"

"Ah" said Patrick nodding sadly, "like many priests he became frustrated with his diminishing status and ashamed of the widespread corruption within his profession, and turned to the gin. At least that's what he tells me. The Hierarchy retired him to Cork where he realised his childhood ambition to breed show horses. I believe they are of a high standard. He goes on the dry during the winter but once the summer and the showing season arrives he goes off the head altogether. Because of the distance between Cork and Fermanagh I rarely see him."

"I remember him as a fine looking-fellow – but much younger than you," Thelma said. "There's another thing I want to ask you, what is this 'spearbhean' thing you keep moaning on about when you make love to me? It's getting to me not knowing what it is."

"Well now," said Patrick smiling lovingly at her, "The spear-bhean is known in Nordic mythology as well as in Irish. The Norsemen called her the Ice Maiden. Spear in Irish means sky and bean is a woman. She's blonde like yourself. I have a special feeling for her because she visits me in the night while I am asleep. Just when I get excited about being close to her I wake up and she vanishes. These past twenty years you and she have been the same. But you know, I don't think this lady will be bothering me any more."

Thelma's whole face smiled at the end of the last sentence and Patrick felt weak with love for her. And then the taxi arrived and she picked up her handbag. As she had done when she had left him by Albert's graveside, she reached up and lightly brushed her lips against his. "Goodbye Sharpening-stone," she quipped gaily. "I'll be down again next Monday. I have to attend a meeting of the Lough Erne Preservation Society. The time will be the same," and she was gone.

* * *

Heather did a jig in the hallway while holding a letter in
her hand. Suddenly she tore up the stairs and burst into
her mother's bedroom. "Mum! Mum!" she cried, "Will you
please wake up!" Olive shot upright in her bed looking diz-
zy and confused from the effect of the sleeping pills she'd
been taking since Albert's death.

"What on earth is all this about Heather?" she said. "Will
you please calm down!"

"Oh Mum!" screeched Heather, leaping onto the bed and
bouncing up and down, "my results have come and they are
terrific!" She shoved the white sheet of paper into Olive's
face and sat watching her mother's reaction as she quickly
scanned the results.

"Oh darling!" said Olive throwing her arms around her,
"this is wonderful! Your father would have been thrilled.
Oh thank God!" And she hugged Heather again and kissed
the top of her head.

Heather snuggled up to Olive and said, "You know what this
means? I will never, never have to go to school again! And
I can get a job and a car and can go all over the place and
won't have to go bothering you for lifts. I will be able to go
where I want when I want, and I won't have to wait around
till everyone is ready. And I can drive you places instead of
you always having to drive me. And I'll be able to go to the
dances in Kesh and Fivemiletown. Can we make a bonfire
of my school uniform?"

"We'll think about that," Olive said. "Why don't you go downstairs and put the kettle on. We'll talk about it over breakfast."

She leaned back on her pillows thinking that at last here was something to rouse her from the torpor and emptiness of the past weeks, when nothing touched her except the pain of being alone. I'll make an appointment this morning to see Anna Ormsby. She owes me after all I did for her. Heather deserves a decent job. She slowly got out of bed. For the first time since Albert's death there seemed some point in getting dressed, in putting on her make-up, in presenting a smiling face to the world. I'll wear my navy suit, she thought, and the pearls that Albert gave me for our last wedding anniversary.

Thinking of what she would say to Anna, she went downstairs to prepare breakfast.

* * *

Olive was greeted in the offices of C. & C. Ormsby by a cheerful secretary. "Good morning, Mrs. Elliot. Miss Ormsby is expecting you. Isn't it a beautiful day!"

"It is indeed," replied Olive as she was shown into Anna's office.

Anna Ormsby was something of an enigma to the members of the closely-knit Protestant community of Sydare. Brown-skinned and good-looking in a masculine sort of way, she swam daily in Lough Erne. She attended church regularly and when she was not worshipping God, she worshipped the sun. She went alone on package holidays to warm places, taking lots of books in her suitcase. She lived on her own and cycled to and from her office. She had a dog that she adored and walked for an hour each day. Her short affair with the Fenian had shocked the few who knew about it. She wore a tweed skirt that needed pressing and a sweater that an experienced knitter would recognise as having been knitted by herself – and not too well at that. But her welcome was warm as she stood to shake hands with Olive and show her to a chair.

"Do sit down," she said. "I have to say, Olive, you are looking well. By the way, I am hoping to have Probate taken out next week and that will free your money up."

"Actually," said Olive, "that is not the reason why I'm here. I'll come straight to the point. Heather needs a job. She has just got the results of her exams and they are pretty good. I would appreciate it if you could find some work for her to do here." She waited while Anna thought for a moment before saying, "I suppose she has suitable results in typing and English, has she?"

"Oh yes!" replied Olive confidently. "She did really well in those. She studied very hard these past two years and even had grinds for six months prior to the examinations. She actually surpassed the grades her teachers thought she'd make. And I would have to say that she's a good girl. She never gave me a moment's bother. She's modest and intelligent. And she doesn't have a boyfriend," she added.

Anna considered again and then asked, "When could she start?"

"Well," said Olive moving to the edge of her seat, "she could start on Monday if that would suit. Would you like her to bring a character reference from the Rector?"

"That would be fine," said Anna, "and could she please also bring a copy of her results and a current CV?"

"Of course!" said Olive relaxing.

"Her wages will be controlled by the Bar Council," continued Anna, "and I'm afraid I don't have the details to hand. Just a moment. I will ask Ruth." She picked up the receiver and spoke to her secretary. Olive sat quietly thinking about Anna. She was the doyenne of the Fermanagh Bar and the scourge of the Fenians. But she was fair and was treated with respect by all, and she would do just fine as Heather's employer. Olive was content and believed herself lucky that she hadn't had to rake over any old coals to secure a position for her elder child. She felt that she had achieved much in a short space of time. Albert would have been proud of her.

* * *

At his desk on Tuesday, Jamieson tapped on his computer to release PAYE and PRSI details on all people engaged in counter-terrorism. He mentioned to his secretary that he had been called to visit his mother. He asked her to take any messages and to say that he would return the calls on the following day.

He took the information to his apartment in Maida Vale and worked on the details of his role, explaining how ill his mother was and the fact that she only had twelve months to live – or maybe even less. When the work was completed, he took the tube to Kensington Palace Gardens and walked to the embassy with the Hammer and Sickle flag leaping about gaily in the breeze. He ran up the stone steps and shoved the long brown envelope through the wide letter-box.

He was glad to get that over. Taking a quick glance over his shoulder to check that he was not being followed, he hurried to the tube station. He had to get to see his mother quickly as she got tired after six o'clock. He ran up the stairs from the platform and bought flowers for her from the flower seller at the exit onto the street.

He took a taxi to the Wimbledon Hospice and walked into the familiar, well-populated ward. His mother was thrilled to see him. She looked frail and gaunt. He remembered how she used to be – a well-rounded, pleasant-looking woman who dressed well. She was loving and caring and fun to be with. She was a great fan of Patsy Clyne and used to sing Crazy out of tune but with great gusto. Jamieson felt sad as he put his arms gently around her wasted body to embrace her. He laid her back tenderly on her pillows. Now she was ridden not only with cancer but also with guilt. She smiled wanly at her son and said, "Thank you for the lovely flowers. Sorry to be such an awful burden to you, Graham."

Jamieson was frustrated. How could he ever explain to her that he wanted with all his heart to repay her properly for his upbringing and for all the love and affection that she had shown him? He wanted to tell her that he loved her for her bravery in rearing him all on her own. But he could not express himself and so he simply took her hand and said, "Hush, Mother. You are no burden to me at all." But still, the bills in the hospice were a desperate worry to him and he hoped that none of the staff would mention the arrears he owed during his visit. As she lay with her eyes closed he watched her and thought, I cope badly with her pain and suffering. I couldn't have been a doctor. Blast bloody Whicker and her love affair with the Faulklands. She spent all that money unnecessarily when it could have gone towards the welfare of the people here. If only I could afford better for her.

The doctor arrived with a nurse. He said, "Doesn't your mother look well today!" The sick woman opened her eyes for a moment and she smiled weakly at him. Amazing, thought Jamieson, how this man lies.

"Might I have a word with you Mr. Jamieson?" the doctor asked. They went into the corridor together while the nurse made the patient comfortable. "I am sorry to say that your mother has gone down a lot this week. I have increased her morphine but she has lost a great deal of fluid. All I can say to you is to be prepared. Things do not look good."

Passing the office on his way out, the secretary beckoned to him to come inside. "Your bill, Mr Jamieson, is slightly in arrears," she said sternly. "One thousand pounds actually. We did receive your cheque for five hundred, and thank you. Every little helps, but the Government is reducing its subvention next month. It isn't right what's happening," she said, softening slightly.

Bloody sure it's not right, he thought angrily as he marched out onto the street.

All the way back to Maida Vale he considered that if only he had married he would have been able to share his frustrations with a wife. His mother had been right all along. He should have married. Then he could have given her the grandchildren she always wanted. No, he thought finally, I am too selfish. No woman would have put up with me. And on this note he let himself into his apartment remembering ashamedly, for he had forgotten for about ten minutes, that the doctor had told him that his mother could not live for much longer.

Three days later, Jamieson was woken early by the telephone ringing. With his heart pounding, he allowed it to ring five times before picking up the receiver. He swallowed before saying a dry hello.

"May I speak to Mr. Jamieson please?" said a well-tutored female voice. It is nothing to do with my mother, he thought with relief. The voice continued, "My name is Fiona and I am speaking on behalf of Mr. Wilmsloe of Consolidated Insurance. He invites you to Clintons in the Strand for lunch at one o'clock today."

"Thank you," replied Jamieson, "I will be there."

"You will be brought to his table when you arrive," Fiona said.

"Thank you," said Jamieson again, hanging up. "That's good," he thought. Lunch taken care of today! I could do with a good lunch at someone else's expense. Probably wants to sell me insurance, the poor fool."

He dressed carefully and as he strolled up the Strand he said to himself, I am buying no more cover no matter how hard this Mr. Wilmsloe tries! But I'll get a good lunch out of him anyway!

Mr. Wilmsloe stood to shake hands with him and then said, "May I call you Graham?" "My God," thought Jamieson, "this man has his homework done." Wilmsloe went on, "How is your mother?"

"I'm afraid she is slipping away quite quickly," responded Jamieson.

"I want to get to the point straightaway," said Wilmsloe. "I invited you here today as result of a letter you delivered to some Associates. They said that they were so impressed with the quality of the information it contained, that they have instructed me to give you this envelope. They have also looked after the arrears at the Hospice and have had your mother moved to a private room. They insist on meeting all her future bills and have organised a very fine consultant to visit her." Jamieson was speechless. But when Wilmsloe ordered up the bottle of Chablis 92 and a Chateau Neuf du Pape to follow, he got his voice back. He ordered cooked oysters Florentine because he was told that the chef was Sardinian and that they were his forte. He then had consommé and then lobster Thermidore. He mentally patted his full stomach and then helped his digestion with more and more wine. He was quite drunk when the Martel Cordon Bleu arrived. He excused himself from the table and went to telephone his secretary. He explained that something important had come up and asked her to deal suitably with any problems. Returning to the table he smoked two good cigars and drank three brandies. Wilmsloe finally asked for the bill and paid with a gold American Express card. Jamieson accepted Wilmsloe's business card and agreed that if he had any other business he would contact him no matter what the hour. He crawled carefully into the taxi that had been ordered for him, and as he travelled home he opened the big brown envelope. He counted five thousand pounds in twenty-pound notes.

Once inside his apartment, with the stress and financial pressures suddenly lifted and his system filled with good food and wine, Jamieson went to bed and slept well.

IV

The main street of Ballinasup looked resplendent in red, white and blue Union Jacks. They were billowing from every house in town, lording it over the Ballyfia Accordion Band, which was belting out "Give me that Old Time Religion. It's good enough for me." The choir of the Free Believers Church from Ballyfia was dressed completely in white with matching bonnets, and Vanguard scarves on which were stamped the Red Hand of Ulster. They sang lustily as they marched up the street past Heather and Florence on their way to the soccer pitch. A giant marquee had been erected there by the local elders, chief of whom was John Logan, of the Killskerry Group for the purpose of the Revivalist Meeting that would soon begin. The whole aim was the proselytising of younger members. The marchers were led by big Shane Glasgow, who was six foot four inches in his stocking feet. He was enormously built with a voice that was both deafening and compelling. He had charisma. When he got emotional his followers were moved, and when he roused them they were truly roused. Hecklers got their just deserts. He was damning and dismissive of them and his followers were proud of him for it. He detested the Roman Catholic religion. He came roaring up the street, "Ballinasup will fight and Ballinasup will be right!" and the crowd roared its approval. Stressing each syllable he yelled, "All graven images will be burned!" In each hand he held three crucifixes, "and I will burn these myself in the marquee this evening! God Save the Queen!"

At this point, the Reverend Willie McNutt, who was marching beside Shane, took this as his cue and, pressing the microphone to his lips sang, "God save our Gracious Queen, long live our noble Queen, God save the Queen." The crowd joined in and his voice was smothered.

As the last syllable was sung, Big Shane took to his roaring again. "We will now march up the Queen's highway to the marquee and please march in step!" The crowd obeyed and proudly held their heads high, like those who know they are superior always do. Heather and Florence fell in step and joined the rear.

When it reached the marquee the crowd piled in, but already the front seats were taken up by the Ballyfia people and the VIPs. The main bulk was left to stand. Willie McNutt leapt with alacrity onto the stage and grabbed the microphone.

> *Will your anchor hold in the storms of life,*
> *When the clouds unfold their wings of strife?*
>
> *When the strong tides lift, and the cables strain.*
> *Will your anchor drift or strong remain?*

And the crowd, knowing the chorus well, joined in with volume and sincerity,

> *We have an anchor that keeps the soul*
> *Steadfast and sure while the billows roll,*

Fastened to the rock which cannot move,
Grounded firm and deep in the Saviour's love.

Heather and Florence joined in the singing and swaying. They had learned this hymn at Sunday School and it was a great favourite of theirs. The four verses and the four choruses gave Big Shane time to shake hands with his flock and welcome newcomers. As "...in the Saviour's love" was being sung for the last time, he flung himself up onto the stage, frothing at the mouth and the crowd was silenced. He opened his throat and bellowed,

"Old Red Socks is at his dirty tricks again! We are betrayed by Whitehall, surrounded by traitors and their fellow travellers! I am being followed by MI5! This is true my friends, because a senior official in the Northern Ireland Office is a member of this Church! As long as you have the Free Believers Church fighting for Protestantism and the integrity of Ulster, God will not let us endure this battle on our own!"

The crowd agreed wholeheartedly. He waited for them to become silent and then continued, "We shall overcome the Fenians! We shall overcome the followers of Rome who take their direction from Old Red Socks!" A few followers broke into, "We shall Overcome", but it was not the right moment and they soon became silent. "We have beaten O'Neill," he yelled, "and Lundy and that snivelling Faulkner! And we've beaten Lord Chichester Clarke and Wilson, Heath and Whicker! We will fight to destroy any Anglo-Irish agreement and send those harlot civil servants back to Dublin with their tails between their legs!"

61

The crowd roared its compliance with all that was being said. "We have the men in mid-Ulster and here we can rely on one of our own, our singer!" he said with pride, pointing to Willie McNutt, who was beaming. "He will organise the fight from here to drive these infidels from the land of God our Beloved! The God-fearing people of north Antrim will be led by myself, and from the hinterland of east Belfast, our God-fearing George Williamson will do what is necessary! And furthermore," he added, "we will not be on our own. I have promises from Pastor Greene that our kith and kin in Scotland will not be found wanting! Let us pray to the Lord to watch over us as we go from strength to strength and finally cross our own Jordan! We must appeal to our beloved police force which is being harassed and shot in Drumree, and be thankful to our brethren from Monaghan and Donegal who gather with us in our confrontation in Portglentoo every year!"

Big Shane shook with emotion, and the effort of all this sincerity was visible in the beads of sweat that rolled down his temples. "We are proud of them," he said, "for marching down the Queen's highway in defence of our civil and religious liberties! We will never surrender to the IRA at Drumree Church, who hide behind the women and throw stones at our officers and constables! A Protestant Police Force for a Protestant People! That's what Carson set up to protect us from, heretics who we'll lock up in jail to await the Judgement Day. And what a Judgement Day that will be, my friends! The Lord will call them into eternal flames and perdition!" He threw his enormous hands to the sky and the crowd loved him. Mustering all the strength of his

enormous body and drawing it from his very toes he bellowed, "God Save Ulster!"

The crowd clapped until their palms were stinging. From
his sitting position he asked for a silent collection, and the
people willingly put their hands in their pockets for the
money that was expected from them. Led by Willie Mc-
Nutt's lovely voice, they sang while they paid out and they
were happy and confident.

Restored, Big Shane got to his feet again and asked those
who wished to be saved to approach him. People surged
forward. His voice once again in order he thundered, "Do
you renounce Satan and all his works? Do you? Do you?"
The future converts got very excited and they roared and
screamed that they did. They most certainly renounced the
Devil and all his works.

Satisfied, he thundered again, "Well then, do you renounce
the Harlot of Babylon?" The people roared and shouted until they were hoarse that the Harlot of Babylon was totally
renounced by them. Big Shane appeared relieved at having
made them see the error of their ways and so, to maximise
the effect, he dipped one of the crucifixes in methylated
spirit and set fire to it, yelling, "Do you renounce graven
images? Do you renounce graven images?" As he threw
the burning crucifix into a metal container and added the
other two to it, the converts were beside themselves. Some
of them were even crying. They sobbed that the graven images were ever so totally renounced. And Big Shane called
on God Almighty to draw them to his side.

Florence was transfixed to such an extent that Heather had to pull at her to get her attention. "Come on out of this," she urged. "We've heard enough of this rubbish. Next thing he'll be looking for another collection," and she pushed Florence out of the marquee in front of her. Once out on the soccer pitch, they both took deep breaths of fresh air and felt better. They had been standing for a long time and they were tired. Walking towards the gate, they met Mr. Henry, who seemed pleased to see them both, but especially Heather.

After he had shaken hands with them he said to Heather, "Miss Ormsby tells me that you have started work with her? Good girl! You made a wise choice! What I want to know is, if you would be interested in working at night with the Greenfinches?" As Heather thought for a minute he continued, "It's very easy work you know. Mostly nights and weekends. You could easily take home eighty-five pounds a week. If you did decide you could manage it, you would be keeping up a fine tradition." Heather was not sure what to say, so Mr. Henry said, "Think about it, my dear. Call me in the morning. If you decide to join the Greenfinches, I will help you to fill in the forms." Heather protested that that would be a lot of bother for him. "Not at all!" he said. "I'd be delighted. I'd simply stay on after closing time to help you. It wouldn't take long. Phone me in the morning then! Goodbye girls!"

* * *

Since beginning her job, Heather had taken out a loan and bought a perfectly serviceable Datsun. It was red and she was thrilled with it. "No smoking in my car!" She nudged Florence in the ribs. "Anyway, if Mummy found out that you were smoking she would kill you!"

Florence put away her packet of ten Marlboro Lights and her matches. "You're a spoil sport!" she retorted.

"What'll I do about the Greenfinches?" Heather asked her.

"Sure join them," said Florence shrugging her shoulders. "What've you to loose? It would help with the car repayments wouldn't it?"

"You're right," answered Heather. "I'll give old man Henry a ring in the morning."

She swung into the car park of the Parklands Hotel. "We'll have a glass of cider each," she said, "and if you tell Mummy, you're dead!" Florence assured her that she wouldn't if Heather kept her mouth shut about the cigarettes. The pact was made and the two of them went inside.

There was singing in the bar. Florence looked over to the corner and nudged her sister. "Well, look who's playing the piano! If it isn't Sharpening-stone! And what's he playing? The Northern Lights of Old Aberdeen! God! D'ya know I'd fancy him if he wasn't so old!"

Heather checked her. "You know Mummy hates it when you call him Sharpening-stone," she said. "I once asked her how he came to get that name and she told me it wasn't nice and would say no more."

"Aunt Thelma gave him the name," laughed Florence. "Coming from her I am sure it has something to do with sex."

"Will you behave yourself!" said her sister.

By this time Patrick Maguire had spotted the two girls and beckoned them to come over to him. He continued playing and called to the barman. "What'll you have girls?" he asked. "I'm on the stand."

"Two glasses of cider, please," said Heather as she and her sister sat down close to the piano.

"Do you play here for money, Patrick?" asked Florence. Heather was mortified. Patrick wasn't the slightest bit put out.

"Yes, I do. Every Friday. Eight to twelve. Do you know, you are two of the prettiest girls in the county!"

"Gee thanks!" said Florence, grinning. Patrick decided she was a flirt. "You did well at Daddy's funeral?"

"I did, thanks. But it was off broad backs it was coming. I never went looking for the money. People kept pushing it at me and my father always told me never to refuse it. It was an awful day and I got a cold out of it."

He noted that Heather was not saying much and leaned towards her whispering in her ear, "Saw you going into the marquee. Your father would not have liked it."

"I know," Heather answered simply, "but I wanted to see for myself and Florence was all on for it."

"She would be," said Patrick, shaking his head a little. "I heard that singing bigot letting it go with that fine voice he has. That pair of cowboys have got a lot of people into a heap of trouble. They say they don't agree with violence, yet every terrorist knows the colour of the wallpaper in both of their sitting rooms." Heather had to laugh at this last remark – even though it was against her will. She really liked Patrick Maguire and couldn't for the life of her think why her mother was so stand-offish with him. He went on, "Those bucks are just very bad news – but I don't want to talk about them any more. How's your mother bearing up?" Heather said that her mother had good and bad days but felt that she was coping pretty well. "And, by the way," said Patrick, "I really like your new Datsun. It suits you! How is your Aunt Thelma getting along? I never see her at all. She's a fabulous-looking woman, don't you think?"

"Pity then," said Heather, "that I didn't take after her."

"Ah come on now!" said Patrick, "You're beautiful too, just in a different sort of way. But here, I must get back to my piano or I'll get the sack. If the two of you come in again next Friday night we'll have more craic." He began to play, It's a Long Way to Tipperary, and Florence joined in. Heather was thinking about what Patrick Maguire had said about her father and their going to the marquee. Another two glasses of cider arrived and they smiled their thank yous at Patrick who winked back. When they'd finished the cider they went home.

* * *

Heather tidied up her desk in the office and went to collect her jacket and handbag. She was excited about joining the Greenfinches and was looking forward to having her forms filled in. She and the rest of the staff parted company in the car park and she drove her car to Mr. Henry's premises. He owned Henry Motors.

Archie Henry walked across the forecourt to meet her. "Good girl!" he said. "You're very punctual," and he shook her hand. "We're just finishing up. Please go right through to my office and pour yourself a cup of coffee. I'll be along in just a moment." Heather looked around his office while she sat drinking the coffee. He was obviously pretty wealthy. The office was super. She stood up to look at the framed photographs of Mr Archie Henry and his wife and children, which were all over the walls. "A good family man!" she reckoned.

When he finally came in, he was carrying a sheaf of paper, which he laid on his desk. He patted a chair and asked her to come and sit beside him. "OK," he said, we'll get all of this organised. Now for the usual questions. Date of birth? Address? Telephone number? Mother's maiden name? Have you got a current driving licence? Who are your referees? What schools did you attend? And your re-ligion is Church of Ireland? Relatives in police regiments or prison services? Any convictions for criminal activity? Right then. That's the bulk of it. Would you please sign here, and here, and here." Obediently Heather signed and then the situation changed.

Archibald Henry laid his hand on her thigh and said, "What a lovely young girl you are," and Heather saw the lecherous look in his eye. He told her that his wife no longer loved him as he slid his soft, white, disgusting hand under her skirt and up between her legs. He tried to kiss her with his flabby lips. For a moment she was frozen to her chair and then she got the strength of ten women. She drew her hand back, closed her fist and with all her might hit him an almighty crack on the bridge of his nose. She ran screaming from the office.

Heather did not remember getting into her car, nor starting the engine, nor driving to the Parklands Hotel. She came to her senses as she washed her face in the warm water in the bathroom there. She was shocked and disgusted. She leaned against the wall and began to think. Who could she tell? She'd have to tell someone or burst. And she wanted revenge on Archie Henry, pillar of the Church, family man, esteemed citizen. She realised that Aunt Thelma was the one. "She'll look after that dirty old lecher for me," and she got out her address book to get Thelma's number and called her on the hotel telephone.

Thelma was not at all surprised at what Heather had to tell her. She felt sorry for the girl but told her to calm down and not to worry in the slightest. "That Archie Henry has been a dirty old man for years!" Thelma told her. "He's tried that on lots of young girls and the pity is that not one of them gave him a crack in the balls to sicken him. He's been preaching religion since time began, Bible in one hand, cock in the other. Just don't worry darling," she soothed. "Your job with the Greenfinches is secure. I'll see to that. And isn't it your birthday next week? I'll send you a hundred pounds. Get yourself some nice clothes. Now go home and not a word to your mother. Anyway, I'll be down next Monday. I'll tell Mr Henry never to as much as look at a family member of mine again. I'll also check to see if he's driving home sozzled after golf. It's time the bugger was caught."

Heather smiled smugly as she crossed the foyer on the way back to her car. "Aunt Thelma will stitch him up good," she smirked. The thought added two inches to her stature as she stepped lightly across the car park.

* * *

Heather, believing that she looked like a model, haughtily minced down the steps into the All Seasons Bar in Enniskillen. Now that she was well-established in her job, she felt much more sure of herself. She had decided, in the office, that a little drink before going to meet Major Benson at the local UDR headquarters would be a good idea.

Looking around and suddenly feeling self-conscious, she was relieved to see Patrick Maguire smiling at her from where he sat at the bar. She eased onto the barstool next to him, put her handbag on the counter and sat grinning at him and swinging her legs. "What'll it be, Heather?" he asked, obviously pleased to see her.

"A glass of white wine would be lovely!" she answered.

"I trust," said Patrick with curiosity, "you haven't attended any more Christian gatherings other than your own Church of Ireland services?"

"No, I haven't," said Heather firmly, blushing just a little.

"You are well served by your Rector and Bishop, you know," Patrick continued. "They are two compassionate, well-read, intelligent gentlemen. I was at Trinity College at the same time as they were there." Heather looked at him with total disbelief as he went on, "They both got distinctions in their M.A.s – not like that other guy who got his illusionary degree from some Bible-thumping pseudo campus in America."

He was prepared to say more. Heather could see that. But she quickly interrupted him to say, "You went to Trinity?"

"Oh yes," said the gravedigger matter-of-factly. "I got a scholarship to read Law there during the fifties. It was great! I loved every minute of it. I was there for two-and-a-half years. Unfortunately, I never finished. This uncle of mine in the States took sick, and, as my brother was about to study in Maynooth for the priesthood I had to say goodbye to the Law degree. His vocation was much more important than mine so I was the one who had to go to the States and look after his affairs." Heather looked shocked.

"I didn't really mind," Patrick continued, shrugging his broad shoulders. "I had a great old time on the other side of the Atlantic for five years. The Law just wasn't to be. When I came home for my brother's ordination, didn't my father keel over and die! I had to weigh in here then. I tried to persuade my mother to sell out the farm and move to a smaller place, but she wouldn't hear tell of it. That woman had pride in her home and the farm, she was totally upset by my father's death and had no ability whatsoever to see things in the long term. Her biggest wish was that my brother, the priest, should always have a decent place to come home to. I was, naturally, said by her. She was a great mother to us and I wanted to do what pleased her most."

Heather was nodding understandingly while Patrick told his story. "And what happened then?" she asked.

"Well," he said, smiling wanly, "my mother lived for ten years more. When she died, my brother and I had a long discussion and it transpired that what he wanted and what she had wanted for him were two totally different things. He was happy for the farm and house to be sold. He had no notion of ever coming back to it. His life was, by that time, in Cork. Do you know it took me two years to get the place sold! I had definitely put Law out of my head by that stage. I bought the house in Monument Hill then, and that's where I've been ever since."

"But are you happy Patrick?" Heather wanted to know.

"Ach, I am, I suppose," he replied. "I play a bit of golf and I have a small boat on the lake. I have no one to answer to. My only responsibility is to myself. I'd have liked to have married and had children but I suppose I'm a bit odd and no one woman wanted me."

"Well now," said Heather, itching to get back to the thing that had so taken her by surprise, "I never knew you studied Law at Trinity. Did many people know?"

"Your father knew. He used to visit me while I was a student. I thought the world of him!"

"I know," said the girl quietly and then they were both silent for a time. Patrick, drumming his fingers on the counter, brought up the topic of Shane Glasgow again. "Your father had no time for him. He thought he was like the Grand Old Duke of York." Then Heather and he said in unison,

> The Grand Old Duke of York,
> He had then thousand men.
> He marched them up to the top of the hill
> And he marched them down again.
> And when they were up they were up,
> And when they were down they were down,
> And when they were only half –way up
> They were neither up nor down.

"Yes," laughed Patrick, "did you know that that buck had ten thousand men up in the Tyrone mountains waving gun licences?" Heather burst out laughing and her companion was delighted to see her do this. So many young people who had been affected by the Troubles, as she had been, were now paranoid and reactionary. "Will you have another glass of wine?" he ventured.

"No," she said, "I have a good job now. Let me buy you one."

After the barman had brought the drinks Patrick said urgently, "Heather, I want to say something to you that I said to your father fifteen years ago – and had he listened to me then, your mother would likely not be a widow now."

"Say on," she answered with interest.

"Now that you are feeling wounded, you will be approached by people asking you to join the Regiment. They're not brave enough to join themselves but they believe that you will be willing. They will point out that your family has a tradition of service. Be careful. All armies through the centuries, whether they were Assyrians, Carthaginians, Roman Crusaders, Holy Romans and, more recently, Japanese Nazis have two things in common – conquest and rape. I repeat, if you do think it necessary to join, be careful. Some of the males regard female soldiers as bed warmers and nothing more. You especially will be vulnerable. Beware of the kindest and most handsome ones. Think about it."

"Aw come on now Patrick!" Heather chided, "Don't you think I can take care of myself?"

"I mean what I say," he replied calmly, "but I am sure you think I have preached enough."

"Well I do that," she said, taking her glass from the counter and tilting it to her lips to finish off what was left in there. She was thinking, "What would this Patrick know about the Regiment! What he says is nonsense!" Looking at her watch she said, "Many thanks for the drink and the chat. It was great to meet someone I knew in here this evening. I must be off. Take care!" And easing herself off the bar stool she waved as she strode away up the stairs.

* * *

Heather collected her car and drove to the Barracks. A large notice on the way in said, "Warning. You are now entering a military establishment." She drove to the barrier and was asked by a military policeman on duty there what her business was. "I have an appointment," she said, "with Major Benson." She produced her driving license by way of identification and the policeman telephoned to confirm her appointment. She was then asked to park behind a black Toyota and wait in her car for Major Benson to arrive and bring her to his office.

She did not have long to wait. Major Benson was tanned, slim, tall, and in his thirties. He strode towards her car and opened the door for her. "How do you do, Heather!" he said, shaking her hand. "Please come with me. There is no need to lock your car here. By the way, I knew your father very well indeed. I was on many patrols with him. He knew the hills, mountains and bogs of Fermanagh like the back of his hand." They went across the courtyard together chatting amicably. She went before him into his office and sat down opposite him at his desk. "Excuse me just one minute, Heather!" said Major Benson, dialling an internal number. "Sergeant Whyte," he said after waiting for a moment, "could you please bring the uniform and beret set aside for Private Elliot to my office. Thank you." He replaced the receiver and got to his feet. "Would you like a cup of coffee?" he asked. When Heather agreed he poured two cups and brought them back to his desk. He settled himself in his chair and looked Heather in the eye. She accepted this eye contact with confidence and he was impressed. "I am sure you will like it here," he said. "There is plenty of fraternising between the NCOs. I am placing you under Sergeant Whyte's tutelage. She will introduce you to your mates and see that you both learn and are happy." Heather nodded and smiled, feeling that she had made the right decision to join the Regiment. Patrick Maguire knew nothing about it.

There was a knock on the door, and in marched, saluting, the ugliest woman Heather Elliot had ever seen in her whole life. She was broad and tall and built like a Clydesdale horse, "except a Clydesdale horse would have a kinder face," Heather thought. Because Heather had been well brought up, and had had instilled in her never, ever to register shock at another human being's misfortune, her face was expressionless. All this was noted by Major Benson. Sergeant Whyte had an unfortunate nose. It was plastered all over her large face as if, during a round of boxing, Cassius Clay had met her full on with her hands dangling by her sides. And then there were her eyes. They were both staring at her nose. "This was," Heather thought, "a face that only a mother could have loved."

The Sergeant handed first the uniform and then the beret to Heather and then, saluting again, asked Heather to follow so that she could be shown her quarters. Heather became slightly confused. She jumped to her feet clutching her uniform, hurriedly said goodbye to Major Benson and raced out of the room in pursuit of the pounding horse that already seemed to be fading into the distance down a long corridor. She caught up with her just as she put her right shoulder to the swing doors of the canteen. Heather put her hand out to hold the door open and, going in, found herself in a room teeming with husky men who were smoking and making ribald remarks to Greenfinches, who answered in the same vein with profanities thrown in for good measure.

Sergeant Whyte showed her to an empty table and barked at her, "Tea? Coffee? Milk? Sugar?" Heather did not want to drink anything, for her bladder was already stretched with the wine and Major Benson's coffee. However, she felt it would be rude to refuse and so accepted coffee. While the Sergeant went off to get it, she sat and looked around her. She recognised a lad from the Secondary Modern. He had been a year ahead of her at school and was called Gilbert Watson. He lived near Killadun. She didn't know he had joined up. He too noticed Heather, for he waved at her in a most friendly way. The Clydesdale came back with a tray and set it down on the table. Settling on one of the many little stools that were all over the floor of the canteen she said, "When we are off duty you may call me Lily."

"Thank you Lily!" said Heather.

"I see," said she, "that you know Gilbert Watson? He's a great lad. Been with us just six weeks and is so ambitious that he has already put in an application for a Corporal. Have to say he's got guts and him only in the door. He works in Stephenson's Butchers and drives a beautiful red Capri. He'd be good for a lift for you." Heather proudly said that she was in no need of a lift, having got a car herself. The Sergeant wasn't really impressed.

Gilbert came over to their table and spoke to Heather. "Nice to have you with us!" he said warmly. "I heard about your new job. No more than myself, you obviously took this on for a top-up to the salary!" He grinned and then said, "I must be off to change because I am on manoeuvres tonight. See you around!"

"Get that coffee down you fast!" said Lily. "We must go to the locker room and get you to fit your uniform on." She leapt up, yanked at her tunic and took off. Again Heather was thrown by the speed at which she pounded away and she felt like a foal as she gambolled to keep up with her Sergeant.

When they got to the locker room, Lily assigned her locker number 315 and then said, "Get that uniform on then!" Heather looked around to see where she could go for a little privacy in which to change her clothes. She saw none and looked at Lily questioningly. "Hurry up!" Lily barked. "I haven't got all evening!" Heather opened the door of the locker and gingerly stepped out of her neat little working suit. She hated being watched but got on with the change as quickly as she could. She put the uniform on, straightened it and stood looking at Lily, waiting for her comments. Lily came towards her to straighten her beret and then, after stroking Heather's cheek with a tenderness from which the girl recoiled, she stood back to get the overall view. "That's grand!" was her pronouncement. "You're on duty now. You must call me Sergeant Whyte. Once you are in uniform there'll be no more Lily!" She pointed out the window. "That's the Parade Ground. You're to be out there in ten minutes flat. There'll be ten of you for instruction and you will be drilled by Sergeant Major Hudson. Get the salute right! He's a devil on the salute – but listen to him well. He's the best in Northern Ireland." And she departed – fast.

Heather locked number 315 and went to the lavatory. With a great sense of relief she came out and washed her hands. She straightened her uniform once again, touched her beret and stepped nervously out into the corridor. Gilbert was waiting for her. He said quickly, "I've two minutes to talk to you before I must be somewhere else. Watch that Lily. She's a dyke! By the way, I'm going to the hop in the Parklands on Saturday night."

"Is that an offer?" Heather asked, pretending she was well used to being asked to go on dates.

"Perhaps it is!" he winked. "I'm gone!"

"That fellow has some cheek!" thought the new Private Elliot, but her heart was pounding. She'd never had a real date before. "I'm as well to go," and she checked her watch and hurried to the Parade Ground.

The handlebar moustache in uniform was lining up nine Greenfinches, and he pointed to an outside position and Heather obediently went to fill it. The drilling started and they were marched up and down, up and down, until Heather wanted to giggle, remembering the nursery rhyme that she and Patrick had recited in the All Seasons Bar a few hours earlier. "At ease!" he finally bellowed and the ten Greenfinches, with no exceptions, thanked God silently. "Right girls," said Sergeant Major Hudson, becoming human, "next week will be more interesting. Weapon practice. Same time, same place. You can dismiss!"

The girls wandered off in groups, leaving Heather a little lost. Then the Sergeant Major said, "Heather! I want to talk to you." She went to him wondering what it was that he wanted to say. "Find the NCOs mess and order me a gin and tonic – and have one for yourself. Sit down and wait for me there. I'm just going to shower. I'll be along in five minutes." When he came back, the Sergeant Major pulled a stool up to Heather's table and sat down. He began, "Your father and I were best friends in the Regiment. How did you enjoy your first evening?" Heather said that she had enjoyed it very much and watched in wonder while he drank his gin in two gulps. He continued, after wiping his moustache carefully, "Many's the night I was with him on manoeuvres. He bloody well knew every nook and cranny in those bogs and mountains – and the people too! How many cups of tea and drops of poitin did we drink together! Ah yes, those were the times! He always got me a bottle of the famous stuff at Christmas for myself. Some old fellow he knew from Shraigh mountain kept a still. I miss your father. I suppose I always will. Anyway Heather, I will be a good friend of yours. You can call on my anytime. Anything I can do to help. You know. I have just one bit of advice for you and you can take it or leave it. Don't look for revenge. It will be hard for you but remember, people from the far right are preaching that there should be civil and religious liberty, while at the same time they agitate and look to degrade those who hold different religious beliefs. On the platforms and in their churches they rant and rave, stirring up young people, terrifying their victims out of their homes, bombing their houses in the middle of the night and all in the cause of civil and religious liberty – some liberty!"

Heather was staring at the table during this one-sided conversation. She felt that this Sergeant Major, Harry, knew that she had been to listen to the Reverend Shane Glasgow. She was now beginning to be furious with Florence for having urged her to go to Ballinasup that day. She looked at Harry and he went on, "Stay away, Heather, from false prophets with their false doctrines and dangerous beliefs. One of them maintains that his reason for vilification comes from Elijah – speaks of Babylon. What can possibly be the relevance in this day and age of people who are centuries dead and cities long in ruins! Stay away from these evil men, I beg you. Anyway," he said, on a more even keel, "how is your mother keeping?" Heather said that her mother was coping pretty well and was keeping busy. Harry said he was glad to hear it. He then said that he had to go and so he and Heather shook hands and left the NCOs mess going in different directions.

Heather had the locker room to herself. She felt weary. What a day it had been! She showered and changed back into her neat little suit and folded her uniform. She left the Barracks and drove home. Olive and Florence were already in bed but not asleep. She said goodnight to both of them and then got quietly into her bed and turned off the light. She lay in the dark thinking of Patrick Maguire's lost

Law degree, her thundering new Sergeant of whom she was to beware, handlebar moustaches, marching and finally she thought of dancing with Gilbert Watson and then she fell asleep.

V

Sean Rose sat in his office in Gardiner Place, Dublin. His telephone rang and he picked up the receiver while tilting his chair backwards. "Oh hi, Boris!" he exclaimed, "How are you? We haven't seen you in Ireland for at least two years! That was some promotion you got! Head of Station, London, no less! Man dear, how you've climbed! You want me to come over right away? I can do that. Of course. Ticket at the Ryanair desk in Dublin? OK. You'll keep me at the Embassy then? Fine! I'll catch the five o'clock. Bye."

He quickly dialled his wife. "Hello Moira! You remember Big Boris? Well, he's just phoned me. Says he wants me in London ASAP. Would you ever pack an overnight bag for me and take a taxi to the airport. Yes, I'm leaving on the five o'clock. You can take the car home. Children OK? Fine. See you at the airport then." He hung up, tidied the papers on his desk, put on his jacket, took the car keys from his pocket, told his secretary he was off to London and would telephone her from there, and left the office.

* * *

"Great to see you Boris!" said Sean Rose, coming forward with hand outstretched to meet the Russian who looked like an enormous wrestler with a grin. "My God, but you look fit! What have you been doing with yourself? I've never been in Kensington Palace Gardens before, you know. It's terrific!"

Boris agreed that he was fit and had been spending time in the gym. He also agreed that Kensington Palace Gardens was a good spot to be in and then he said, "We'll do the business when we get inside," as he ushered Sean into the building. Once inside his office, Boris wasted no time in showing Sean the reason for asking him to come immediately to London. Sean looked at the papers showing the PRSI and PAYEE details on Captain Darcy and his mates and his expression was incredulous.

"My God!" he murmured under his breath. "Where did you get this information? I can't believe it! It's sensational! Let me sit down!" and he sat carefully into the nearest chair, all the time staring at the papers he had in his hand. After a few more minutes, during which Boris watched his reaction, he continued, "These guys are nutcases. What do they think they are at? A full-time Captain and three Lieutenants – the full G7. We always knew that there was a dirty tricks team, but we had no idea it was manned by highly skilled and trained officers. It would seem that G7 are the thinkers, and the Group are the doers, with G7 passing out the guns and selecting targets – and the British taxpayer sustaining and encouraging this lot. You do know, don't you Boris, that we are bound by the decisions of our Ard Comhairle and are now non-military? We do have some renegades who stray away from civil obedience, however. We can touch base with the INLA but they are not as reliable as I would like. It is unlikely that the Ard Comhairle would sanction a retaliatory strike – although we have the men and the material to do it. This, I think, would be better handled by the Provos." He paused for a moment and then Boris took over.

"This," Boris said, is in breach of every international law and ethically a disaster area. Does the Dublin Government have any clue this is going on? Or are they like Nelson, turning a blind eye? To think that a senior civil servant and a Major are involved in this!"

"These," replied Sean, "are probably the same bastards who bombed Monaghan and Dublin, courtesy of the British Exchequer – possibly a throwback to the Littlejohn brothers. Boris, I will personally show these documents to Joe Molloy and let him take over from there." He continued, "I must say that this information scares me. I will Photostat copies for the Provisionals. I'll seal the envelope and deliver it by hand to Belfast. These men will probably arrange a welcoming committee and extract other information. I will just give them sight of this, and let them take their own notes, and return the original to our safe in Gardiner Place."

"Sean," said Boris, "you are a delight to deal with! I have been given one thousand pounds to make sure that you are not out of pocket. Would you like a little drink and I can arrange Olga for you for this evening?" As Sean said yes on both counts, he poured copiously from the gallon bottle of Absolut. Rose, who enjoyed good-quality liquor, sat back and revelled in letting the vodka trickle gently down his throat and relished the warm feeling it gave him. A telephone call was made and a rendezvous set up with Olga. Drink finished, Sean and Boris went out together.

They met Olga at the Embassy and Boris introduced her as his Assistant Secretary. She had had a very active career and had seen service in Budapest and Vienna. She always carried a little Beretta. They sat down to have a drink before dinner. Rose thought her a raunchy female – strong and good-looking with fine teeth and very blue eyes. She dressed with understated good taste and was excellent company. Her English was perfect. Boris had previously explained to Sean that he and Olga would be having dinner together in the suite he had booked for them, and when he had finished his drink he left.

Not too much was eaten by either of them because Olga was very flirtatious and Sean was deeply excited by her. When he went to sit on the couch, she came and sat beside him and, taking her shoes off, she wriggled her feet underneath his backside and grinned at him. Sean put his wife Moira clean out of his mind and without a word he took Olga's hand and led her to the bed. They kissed hungrily as they removed each other's clothes and then, roughly, he took her. The sex they had was fast and cruel. It was driven by lust and it satisfied both of them.

Next morning Sean Rose left for Heathrow, where he caught the 10.30 flight to Dublin. This change from Ryanair to Aer Lingus was tactical. Moira met him and drove him to Connolly Station, where he had to wait awhile before taking the express train to Belfast. He gave his wife nine hundred pounds and told her to put it in a safe place. Putting the remaining hundred in his pocket he kissed her goodbye and went off in search of a stand from which to buy the Irish Times and a biro so that he could do the crossword on the journey. During the flight home he had considered bringing the car to Belfast, but then realised that a Dublin-registered car there would attract RUC attention and so opted for taking the train.

Later, as the train crawled slowly through the outskirts of Belfast, Rose was able to read the graffiti daubed on various walls. "What a shitty city," he mused. At the exit from the train station he hailed a black taxi. "Castlecourt Shopping Centre!" he snapped. When the taxi let him off, he walked the short way to the Sinn Fein Advisory Centre at the bottom of the Falls Road. He circumvented two bulky men who watched him suspiciously, and sidled through a side door.

"Well, if it's not one of the Stickies," said Joe Molloy greasily. "You are very welcome. Seen the error of your ways and come to join us, have you?" The slits Rose made of his eyes in response to this greeting warned Joe to shut up and he preceded him into a back room. Rose immediately asked, "Joe, how many sound men can you get? I have very sensational stuff on me. Where are your Chief of Staff Intelligence Officer and your Quartermaster General? Those two are all I would trust with this. The stuff will have to be read by them, any other way and it would blow the cover of our best man in London if it was leaked. Send taxis to get them. And get them here in thirty minutes for an extraordinary general meeting," he said with determination.

Exactly thirty minutes later, the meeting convened with the two men in question present. Molloy took the chair and said firmly, "I intend to suspend standing orders and have no minutes taken. I welcome a fraternal delegate from Dublin – an ex-member of our Party and Ard Comhairle who sees matters differently from us but, at the same time, I hold him in very high esteem. He and I were imprisoned during the sixties. He comes today," he continued, "with very bad news for us. There has been a widespread breach in our security, which has to be sorted out, and he tells me that a senior civil servant in Whitehall is privy to our secrets. You will be shown the evidence of this and then we will have a discussion.

There was silence in the room while the men read what was shown them and the air was thick with disbelief. "Now," said Molloy, breaking the silence, "you have seen with your own eyes what is a breach of international law. A crowd of thugs, same as the Black-and-Tans in the twenties, funded by Whicker's government and given rank and pay as full-time officers in the service of Her Majesty, that's what they are!" It was plain that he was steaming with anger. "They obviously have no regard for us Irish – or a democratically elected Parliament. We will deal with this problem," he said icily and added, "I express our thanks to our past colleague and wish him a safe return journey to Dublin."

VI

A rchie Henry and Wilfred Silver had just lost three three and six to Dr Black, and Charles Henderson had been beaten overall four and three to play. They had just lost not only twelve pounds, but they had also been knocked out of the Spring League. The drinks, as usual, were on the winners and Archie and Wilfred decided to drown their sorrows at the bar counter. Everybody understood. Four rounds of drink later the rest of the players decided to go home. Archie had one for the road. Wishing the barman goodnight, he went to his black coupe 318 and had difficulty getting the key in the lock. He eventually got his car started and headed towards Temple. Suddenly the road was full of RUC men. Archie pulled up and rolled down his window.

"May I see your driving licence, Sir?" asked the policeman politely. Archie fiddled around in the dashboard and the policeman further enquired, "Do I smell drink from you Sir?"

Archie was incensed. "No!" he snapped.

"Have you taken any drink in the last half hour, Sir?" the policeman continued doggedly.

"You dirty ballocks! Are you trying to tell me I'm drunk?" shouted Archie.

"No Sir", replied the policeman calmly, I am a member of the traffic branch trying to enforce the Road Traffic Act".

Archie yelled, "I'll have you transferred to Crossmaglen or Beleek. The DI and I play golf together regularly".

"Is that so Sir? I must ask you to get out of your car".

"I will in my arse get out!" howled Archie, loosing the run of himself.

"Sir, if you insist on behaving like this, I will call the DI, who fortunately just happens to be here on patrol with us tonight. You can explain to him why you want me transferred to a punishment station". He called the Inspector. "Inspector, I have a man here who says he is a friend of yours. He seems to think that you can wheedle him out of taking a breathalyser test. Also, he has, in front of four officers, intimated that he would intimidate me from enforcing the Road Traffic Act...Sir".

"Archie!" said the Inspector, "will you get the fuck out of that car and blow into the bag, because if you don't you will spend the night in jail".

"Fat lot of good you are!" said Archie belligerently, "I play golf with you three times a week. I contribute to your bloody benevolent fund. I am Worshipful Grand Master of our Loyal Orange Lodge".

"Just shut up!" said the Inspector through clenched teeth, but Archie continued.

"I demand that, as a Protestant person being interrogated by a Protestant police force, I be treated like a dog. This is my first offence. I should be entitled to one free bite".

The Inspector was now tired of the situation. He said to his friend, "I have now done all I can for you. You are insulting this officer". Turning to the policeman he said, "Take this gentleman into custody and remand him. I am sure that the magistrate will take a dim view of his conduct when he appears before him in the morning".

The Inspector knew that Archie was for the chop. He had not even been on call that night. He asked to take Archie to one side, as he was being led away, and then whispered urgently to him, "Listen like you have never listened before. Not only have you made a ballocks of yourself, but you have made one of me as well. You and I were both set up this night. You have to go to jail and appear before a magistrate in the morning. Be careful. Sleep on it. I will have Anna Ormsby with you as soon as possible. You have hurt someone. Be careful. Say nothing and keep on saying nothing. Goodnight Archie!" Archie was dumbfounded.

* * *

"Enniskillen Petty Session. All rise for the Resident Magistrate. Her Majesty versus Archibald Henry".

"I, Inspector Robinson, am appearing on behalf of the prosecution".

"I, Anna Ormsby, am here on behalf of the Defence".

"How do you plead? Guilty or not guilty?"

"Not guilty".

"Proceed"

The policeman of the night before stood and said, "On the twenty-sixth of May, this gentleman was apprehended on Golf Club Road. When asked to breathe into the breathalyser bag he refused to do so and was abusive to me personally".

"Was he wasting your time, Constable? Tell me?" the RM beseeched.

"He threatened to have me transferred to a punishment station – gave me the choice of Beleek or Crossmaglen".

"Tell me more. Were you scared?"

"I was, as I like working in the Traffic Branch".

"Tell me, Constable, why do you like Traffic?"

"My daughter was murdered by a drunken driver".

"Yes, Constable?"

"He told me he was Worshipful Master of some Orange Order and that he knew Inspector Robinson".

"Tell me more?"

"Fortuitously, Inspector Robinson was on patrol with us last night and he advised him to breathe into the breathalyser bag".

"And did he?"

"No, not immediately. He did so when he calmed down after speaking to the Inspector".

"Was he, in your opinion, wasting police time?"

"Oh yes, he was!"

"Tell me more?"

"He was very cross and bitter with Inspector Robinson, mentioning contributions to the benevolent fund, and that this was his first offence".

"Do you believe that this was the first time he had driven, while under the influence of alcohol, from the Golf Course?"

"No. On the night in question we were telephoned by a furious parent who wanted his conduct stopped. She said that he was driving home drunk every Sunday night and she was afraid he would kill someone's child".

"Thank you Constable O'Donnell. What did you say your first name was again?"

"Peadar".

"Thank you, Peadar. If every Constable was as dedicated as you are, we would have safer roads. Tell me by the way, what was the reading?"

"Two-hundred-and-fifty".

"Two-fifty! Are you sure?"

"Yes. The whole patrol read it!"

"Unbelievable!"

The judge, looking out over the top of his spectacles at a pale and stunned Archie Henry, said, " I have no hesitation in convicting you of the offence of failing to provide the requisite specimens when asked. Because you refused to supply a specimen of breath at the roadside I now disqualify you from driving for twelve months and fine you the sum of five-hundred pounds. I take a dim view not only of your lack of co-operation but also of your attempt to influence, prejudicially, an Officer of the Law. Those in themselves are serious offences. Any attempt to pervert the course of justice in my Court would normally be dealt a term of imprisonment – first offence or not. Consider yourself very fortunate not to be heading for Crumlin Road Gaol".

Archie stood trying to find saliva in his mouth to swallow.

No sooner had Rose left the office than Molloy shot into action. He summoned the 'sound' men, addressing them rapidly. "Steenson, you are for Newry! Take Jim and Tony with you! The Quartermaster will arrange small arms for you – to be collected in Dundalk. Take a legitimate car. Low profile. Everything kosher. Deal with it tonight! Do not use the phone under any circumstances. There will be a welcoming committee at the Oriel Hotel on Main Street. Deal with Jamieson and his hood".

The men took the information in silence, knowing that they were running against time. Molloy then turned and said, "Dessie, you are for Belduff. Take Mick and Tom. O'Moore's bar is your venue. The Quartermaster will have you fitted out there. No guns until you meet. Niall, take the red fellow and his buddy. Doolin is your destination. Lake of the Ghosts will be your spot. These men are to be treated as spies. They are soldiers out of uniform, carrying out acts of murder and violence in Monaghan and Dublin. You must get them to give you the names of their two sleepers. Darcy must be lifted first so that it will look like he has broken under cross-examination. Three hours after he has been picked up, I will phone the three locations with the word to let all systems rip".

Dessie, known as the Fox, returned to Michaelstown and called around to Mick's place. "We have a job to go to in Belduff" he said easily. "Get ready. Never mind the tiling in McQuillan's" he said as Mick protested. "I can't tell you what it's about at the minute but do you think we can borrow the Nissan from your friend Frank? We need a light car. I have a clean licence. Make sure it's taxed and insured. The Black Bastard would hold us up all day and enjoy it".

Twenty minutes later, the Nissan was filled with diesel and was on the M1. "Do you know what", said Mick, "we'll go by Enniskillen. The road's much more scenic and we can look at the lake for twenty minutes!" The journey was going quickly enough until hunger got the better of them and they pulled up at the little Warrior Queen Hotel in Enniskillen.

They tumbled out of the Nissan and piled into the bar, which was dark after the bright sunlight they had left behind them in the street. A few wasters were scattered around, backs to the bar, eyes either on the television or staring into their black pints, saying little. They shifted their backsides into more comfortable positions on their barstools when the men came in – but that was all. They were more interested in the football on the screen than in the new arrivals. The barmaid smiled cheerfully at Dessie, Mick and Tom, obviously delighted with the little diversion their entrance had created. "Now boys!" she said brightly, "what'll it be?"

"Do you have any bar food, we're STARVING!" burst Mick, settling half of himself on a barstool while keeping one foot on the floor. The other two crowded in behind him. "Anyway, what's your name?" he continued jauntily.

"I'm Roisin!" she said, the smile lighting her face, "and we have all sorts of sandwiches – toasted if you want them that way!"

"Jaysus, pile them up in front of us whatever way you like," said Tom enthusiastically. "Me belly thinks me throat is cut!"

"What'll you have to drink?" she asked.

"Coffee!" they replied in unison. "Now!" added Mick and, as Roisin turned to the percolator, Dessie eyed her up and down. She was slim and wore black jeans with a loose green sweater over them. But what was most striking about her after her smile, he thought, was her hair. It was fine, shiny, long to well past her shoulders, and blonde. She is a fine thing! he thought.

"Boys!" she said, turning with the tray and the coffee and all that went with it, "Do you want to eat inside or out? We have tables set up outside by the river."

"Sure we'll go outside," said Mick to her. "It's sinful to be inside on a day like this".

She preceded them outside with the tray and set it down on the nearest wooden table. "I'll go and get your sandwiches now," she said over her shoulder as she left them. They sat down and Dessie poured the coffee from the pot. Tom said, " Well isn't this a grant spot! How come we never knew about it before! "

"For God's sake man!" retorted Mick, "sure we've never been in any pub in Enniskillen in the day." The three stretched their legs out in front of them and thought about the sandwiches. It certainly was a lovely spot. The river ambled restfully by, first passing under the stone bridge with the four arches and then, after several miniscule falls, they watched it disappear from their view by the old mill. There was an elegant ash tree on the opposite bank, and lots of bushes. The grass by the edge of the river had been freshly mown. Birds sang noisily while the odd van and a few cars passed over the bridge. Occasionally a salmon leapt out of the water on its way upstream. They sat there in amicable silence until Roisin reappeared with a mound of sandwiches. She set them down and then stood back, and with her hands on her hips said, "And where are you off to then?"

Dessie answered quickly, "We're off to beautiful Belduff. Do you want to come with us?"

"Ach, sure I'd love to," she answered, "but I have to stay here and earn the few bob for myself." She tossed her hair over her left shoulder with a quick jerk of her head and Dessie loved the way she did it.

"And what about joining us there tonight?" Dessie demanded. "Would you have any way of getting down?"
"I Suppose I would," she replied thoughtfully, "that's if you'd let me bring my friend with me. Sharon has a car."

"Sharon?" Mick interjected, "is Sharon a good-looker like yourself?"

Roisin blushed with pleasure as she said, "She is indeed and she has legs up to her neck! She's fierce tall!"

"God, I love tall women!" said Mick wistfully through a large mouthful of ham-and-cheese sandwich, "but then they're all the same when you toss them."

"I thought your Mammy told you never to speak with your mouth full, you old pig!" said Tom playfully and then, as the thought struck him, he added, "That's you buggers set up for the night – now what about me?"

"Well" said Roisin rather doubtfully, "there's my friend Bridget. She's a bit big and square, but she's good craic."

"How big?" asked Tom.

"This big I suppose," indicated Roisin with arms out-stretched.

" Sure she'll do me the finest", said Tom resignedly. "I like plenty of woman in my arms", and he flung his arms around himself while the others threw back their heads and laughed at his antics.

So the date was made for that evening. It was decided that they would all meet up at the disco in Belduff, and the boys left with full stomachs to complete their journey.

* * *

They looked down over the High Strait and saw the sea at last. Mullan Strand looked stunning in the bright light, as the whipped waves of the Atlantic rolled and flopped onto the clean sand before scratching backwards and starting all over again. "Not far now" said Mick to Dessie, the Fox, "You will soon be telling us your secret".

* * *

Patrick was ready and waiting on Monday. The time had come for Thelma's visit. He had done all she had asked him. Chablis in the fridge, two-dozen smiling oysters open on the kitchen table. He heard the taxi pull up, and taking the cork from the wine he poured her a glass and then went to open the door.

She marched past him, flinging her coat off on the way to the kitchen. "Leading my nieces astray, were you? You'll get jail if you touch Florence" she teased. "Bet you like her more than me!" she said coyly. Patrick went on the defensive and opened his mouth to reply but she stopped him by saying, "I'm being naughty. Give me a kiss and tell me you love me and then give me that glass of wine." She didn't get the glass of wine immediately, for he threw his arms around her, hugging and kissing her and telling her how he hadn't been able to sleep all week for thinking about her. Thelma disentangled herself and said, "Will you go easy Patrick! I'm going to have my wine and oysters before I have you! How much did he charge for the oysters?"

Patrick said, "Three pounds, fifty."

"Oh the bastard!" said Thelma indignantly. "He always charges me five."

"Good enough for you," said Patrick boldly, "because you look rich – ripe for the plucking." She finished her glass of wine and asked for the Gold Label.

"I had trouble getting that," said Patrick proudly.

"I knew you would have!" she replied smartly. She was testing, always testing. She kissed him on the side of the cheek and he felt desperately excited. "Don't be previous," she whispered in his ear. "I am not going upstairs until I have finished the oysters, a glass of brandy and a few glasses of wine!"

So Patrick and she settled themselves at the kitchen table and the talk turned to why the vast majority of the nationalist community was so hostile to the police. Thelma wanted to know. Patrick said it was an awkward question but he'd tell her what he thought. He explained that when he read the local papers none of the court cases appeared to deal with Unionists. It was the nationalists who took the rap. He told her that he knew that a chap called Willie Evans had been breathalysed four times already. But he also knew that this same man would leave the Coin Bar as full as a shuck on Friday night next, and nothing would be said or done about it. "After the Drumree incident last year," he told her, "only nationalists were before the courts. It did not matter that the local draper and hotelier were diverting marching bands to disrupt traffic on the Queen's Highway, as they call it themselves. Only McManuses, Maguires and O'Donnells were charged. It is also felt that the twenty people, mostly innocent pensioners and three teenagers, who were killed in the mid-Ulster region, were killed by the Local Volunteer

Force, with the active connivance of the RUC. Also the raid on Cappagh. The police are known to have made the way clear for them."

Thelma was thinking. "One more thing," she said, as she seasoned her oysters with Tabasco, Yorkshire Relish and a squeeze of lemon, "how do you see Northern Ireland panning out?"

Patrick frowned and considered the many books on the shelves in his kitchen before answering. Standing up and reaching for his copy of Hansard he said, "Maybe you'd be interested in what Churchill had to say in 1922?" Thelma ate while he thumbed through the pages, laid the book on the table open at the appropriate page, and sat down to read. "This is a great quote," he murmured, nodding.

"Well read it then," she said, sucking her fingers.

He began, "'The whole map of Europe has changed. The position of countries has been violently altered. The modes of thoughts of men, the whole outlook of affairs, the grouping of parties, all have encountered violent and tremendous changes in the deluge of the world. But as the deluge subsides, and the waters fall short, we see the dreary steeples of Fermanagh and Tyrone emerging once again. The integrity of their quarrel is one of the few institutions that have been unaltered in the cataclysm that has swept the world.'"

Patrick closed the book quietly and looked at Thelma for approval. She drew up the left side of her mouth wanly and nodded. "So what will change?" she asked, shrugging her shoulders.

"I may be wrong," he said slowly, "but I see a future Prime Minister, probably Labour, calling in the leader of the Unionist party, explaining to him that he is not putting up with the continual haemorrhage of money, all wasted on security. He will point out that it is with reluctance that he has had to adopt this stance, but that he has been backed into this position by intransigent politicians. He will have to support the ballot, and private polls show that the United Kingdom as a unit will support the break-up. The genuine citizens will vote that a reduction of military support for Northern Ireland will mean a reduction in taxation, and they will vote with their pockets.

"But what about the Tories!" she cried. "Ben Essex is known to have said all this to you-know-who. And then your man didn't listen and accused Essex of shouting at him. Imagine shouting at that dirty eejit! This is probably a long way away, and talking about it is putting me off my oysters and Chablis. Help me to finish them and then let's go to bed."

* * *

Dessie, Mick and Tom made their way to O'Moore's Bar in Belduff. Big Jim met them at the door and went upstairs with them. They went into a large room and he welcomed them and asked them what they would have. They could not admit to having had coffee and sandwiches so they said they would have just coffee. "We're on active service so we can't have a drink".

Dessie added, "Actually we're waiting for a phone call to come here for us from the Quartermaster General."

"Enough said," nodded Big Jim understandingly. "By the way, were you watching Down play on UTV on Sunday? Did you see Mickey run in the goal and six points? Jesus, he's some tit! Didn't he show Charlie Thomond how to score!"

"McGill had a great game at midfield," said Mick joining in the conversation.

And they chatted on about the Gaelic match until the phone call came.

VII

C aptain Darcy was polishing his shoes in his small room in Knockbrook Barracks. He was thinking that in two days' time he would be back home in the bosom of his family. He sang after a few drinks, but he wasn't a man for whistling when he felt happy, usually. But in those few moments a bar or two of 'In an English Country Garden' came fairly tunelessly from his pursed lips. He was really looking forward to visiting his mother in Reddich and his sister in Coventry. It was a long while since he had spent any time with them. The latter lived beside the airport and so he decided that he would fly there first. I can take a taxi to Banbury Road, the thought, and being back in nice, neat, homely countryside away from this madness is bound to get me back on an even keel. I'm through with seaside horrors like Belduff and the awful loneliness of the Glens of Leitrim. I'm sick of crossing and re-crossing borders. I'm truly tired of dealing with uncultured, vicious little madmen like Billy and Robin, but above all I am sick and tired of the Irish problem. In fact, I wish I had never got tied up with it in the first place. Damn my initial enthusiasm. I wish I'd been smarter and thought more about where it would get me.

This last burst of thought put an end to the 'English Country Garden' and he tidied up the polish and the brushes and

105

put his shining shoes neatly underneath his bed. I'll go to Hong Kong, he said to himself. That should be far enough away. They'll be after me for the part I played in those last two executions especially. That creepy Jamieson will look after me. He's an odious little man.

Checking that everything in his room was in order, Darcy closed his door behind him and went in search of the Sergeant. "Should my mother telephone," he said, "please tell her that I will be in Reddich in the next few days, but also say that I will return her call in the morning".

* * *

Jamieson was dreaming about big lump sums of money from the Russians when the telephone rang in his office. He absentmindedly raised the receiver to his ear and said, "Department of the Navy, Jamieson speaking!"

"Could you please hold, Mr Jamieson," said a young female voice, "for a call from Dr Williamson."

Jamieson straightened himself and took a deep breath for he knew what he was about to hear. Dr Williamson, using words that came easily to him after years of practice, told Jamieson that his mother had died twenty minutes earlier. He explained that the Chaplain had been with her at the end and that it had all been very peaceful. He consoled Jamieson by saying how fortunate it had been that the two of them had spent some hours together a few days earlier. And he consoled him further by saying that she had gone into a coma shortly after midnight and had not regained consciousness. He did admit to feeling guilty about not having contacted Jamieson so that he could have been there at the end, but redeemed himself by expressing total surprise that she had gone so fast. Jamieson, even though he had expected all of this, felt numb. He was glad that Dr Williamson said he would look after all the funeral arrangements, glad when the conversation ended and totally distraught after he hung up.

* * *

Captain Darcy decided that what he really needed was a drink, so he drove to The Border Inn, a place he visited occasionally, parked his car and locked it. He walked smartly up the incline and in through the double doors. The pub was fairly full so he made his way to an empty spot beside the piano where Titch Travers was playing brilliantly as usual. He was challenged by being very short in stature but had found a successful and lucrative niche for himself in his pianoplaying. His voice was baritone and he was making a good job of 'Old Man River' as Darcy entered.

When Titch had finished and the applause had died down he said into the microphone, pointing at Darcy, "I've been told that the man with the cap over there will sing, 'I'll Take you Home Again Kathleen'! Good man Mike! Up you get. Key of C isn't it?"

"Ah now," said Darcy smiling icily, "I've only just come in. I'll have to have a few scoops first." Titch accepted this and said that he would sing himself until Darcy was ready. He launched into 'On the Street Where You Live', having been yelled at to do so by a raucous female from the back of the pub.

And so the night wore on. Darcy ordered first one vodka-and-coke, then a second and then a third. Invited singers came to the piano, did their stuff and sat down. Applause waxed and waned but Darcy was not asked the second time if he would sing. He was secretly being drugged by having Rohypnol put in his drink. When he passed out, Huge Euge threw him over his shoulder and carried him outside – but few noticed and even fewer cared. (What did annoy the drinkers was that Titch decided he had entertained them enough for the evening and he left too.) Darcy was thrown into the back of a Hiace van, which had previously been parked at the emergency exit, and was driven off into the darkness.

* * *

Near Eisc River he was lifted from the van and taken to a shack with windows blacked out, and which was lit by a hurricane lamp. He came around because he was being roughly shaken and yelled at.

"Wake up Captain Darcy!" the voice kept repeating. "It's time for you to talk now!"

Darcy's head was exploding in bursts each time his heart beat. He felt dreadful. He eyes wouldn't focus for a time, but when they finally did he realised with horror that he had to be face to face with Doctor Death, the most dangerous psychotic in West Belfast. At that time he could not speak, so Doctor Death did all the talking, and the more he spoke the more terrified Darcy became. With little or no inflection, and certainly no feeling, the man said, "You have been captured as a spy. You are an officer serving out of uniform. Your NIC contribution number is CTZ 2649872. Your total pay per month is 2K and following deductions your net pay is one-thousand-seven-hundred-and-fifty-six-pounds-and-forty-three pence. You have served in Hong Kong and Germany. You were activated for G7 work in Northern Ireland. And you," he said, his voice suddenly becoming animated, "you BASTARD, along with The Group and The Ulster Volunteer Force, have been responsible for bombing Monaghan and Dublin along with other fucking acts of murder and mayhem!" He now began to shout, "You have been found guilty by the GHQ of the Provisional IRA!"

Darcy was cringing. Doctor Death continued, smiling and with a much more even delivery, "I, as Captain in this organisation, have got the job of organising your execution! You know, Captain Darcy, as a spy you do not come under the Geneva Convention."

He smiled delightedly and nodded his head slowly up and down. Darcy was horrified. He continued, "I know all the members of G7. They will be picked up in three hours' time and, do you know, you will be blamed for their capture! Actually," he said as a little aside, "your boss has joined us. I will have you killed within the next hour, and you must agree that your death is only proper. Now, the manner of your death is entirely up to you. Listen carefully," he said evenly. "I will tell you this once and once only. If you tell me the answers to my questions immediately, you will be shot in the back of the head. If you lie, those breezeblocks beside you will be dropped on your legs and you will die roaring. You will even beg for us to finish you off telling us everything. I know! I have done this many times!"

He looked questioningly at Darcy who had glanced at the breezeblocks. When Darcy looked at Doctor Death again he went on, each syllable stressed, "Who are your sleepers? I want their names and addresses." Darcy's mouth was completely dry. "Jamieson," he thought, "is a bastard."

Rasping his dry tongue over the dry roof of his mouth he realised that everything this psychotic said was true and that only he knew his own sleepers.

He looked Doctor Death in the eye and croaked out, with difficulty, the request that he be given time to make peace with his God. He was given the time and then he began, "Jonathan Davidson is originally from Doncaster. He has served with the Royal Engineers in Cyprus and the Falklands. He was given an awareness course in Plymouth and has been a sleeper in Northern Ireland for five years. He is know here as Thomas O'Donnell and lives beside the Parochial House in Knockbrook."

At the mention of O'Donnell's name Titch interjected, "I know the hoor. I'd be delighted to give him his come-uppance!"

Darcy went on, "The other one is Barry Dickson – originally from Wakefield in Yorkshire. He has seen service with the Navy in Plymouth and has been living in the caravan park in Belduff. He is six foot tall with red hair and is called Pauric Gallagher."

"I know him too!" said Titch proudly.

Darcy got to his knees as ordered, said his Act of Contrition and a decade of the Rosary. "Thank you Captain Darcy," said Titch simply, "We believe you, and May the Lord Have Mercy on Your Soul!" Putting the gun to the counter-terrorist's head and pulling the trigger, he watched as Darcy keeled over, his brains spilling out on the floor of the shack.

The lorry from the knacker's yard had been backed up to the door of the shack and Darcy's limp body was heaved in on top of the few dead cattle it contained. "Well now," said Titch, "when the rest of the carcasses are thrown in on top, nobody will find the perfidious Albion." Rubbing his hands gleefully he continued, "Let's go fetch O'Donnell and Gallagher. It'll be gas to hear what stories they'll tell! I bet it was Gallagher was responsible for Killygall!"

"Fuck off, Titch!" said Doctor Death. "Dessie, Mick and Tom'll do that job."

* * *

Tom O'Donnell was sitting opposite Dessie, Mick and Tom in O'Moore's bar and had taken full stock of the situation. They had been introduced as footballers staying at the Hollywell Hotel. He was told they had two matches to play. They all wore pioneer pins and looked extremely fit. He smelt danger. It was Thursday. Footballers didn't arrive until Friday evenings. As they left by the front door, he excused himself to go to the lavatory but instead went out the back door and tore down the lane. By the time they were crossing the bridge over the river, Tom was right behind them. As they were passing the Post Office, Tom ducked into the Old Fountain Bar, ordered a pint of Guinness, took his jacket off and sat by the window to drink and watch what was happening. He knew that the alcoholic priest who was Quartermaster General lived up that end of town and he assumed that that was where the boys were going.

Half an hour went by, during which time Tom never took his eyes off the street, except to swallow a mouthful of his pint. As he saw the boys reappear, he put on his jacket and went outside. He followed them at a distance and his heart was beginning to pound. When he saw them turn in to Lowther Road he felt that he had seen enough. He went to the nearest telephone kiosk and dialled a taxi. "They're going to the caravan park," he said to himself. "Not good! Not good at all!"

His taxi arrived. The driver, Miley, was a friend of his. "Where to?" he asked when Tom opened the door.

"Enniskillen," said Tom and he quickly got in.

"Thought you could get picked up there!" said Miley.

"Sure I could," said Tom, "but my sister Theresa is sick and I'll chance it to go and see her."

"OK by me," said Miley and he pushed the accelerator to the floor as he passed the thirty-mile speed limit. Tom relaxed. He chatted to Miley about local matters and the hour went by fairly quickly for him. As they got to the outskirts of Enniskillen, Miley turned his head sideways over his shoulder and asked, "What part of town?"

"The Coin Bar," said Tom. They discussed the pub while they went down Willoughby Place and across West Bridge. Miley drew up at the door.

"That'll be twenty quid," he said. Tom got out the money.

"There's two quid for yourself," he said, "and thanks! I'll probably see you tomorrow." This was a lie, but lies were safer than the truth at this moment.

Tom went straight through the pub and out the back door. He crossed Head Street and Anne Street and walked up to the front door of the RUC station. He entered and went to the front desk. "Can I speak to someone in CID?" he asked. Inspector Ferguson was called. "Inspector Ferguson," Tom said, "can I speak to you in private?" They went upstairs together to a room that appeared to be little used. When the Inspector closed the door Tom said, "I am Lieutenant Davidson from counter-terrorism. I need access to a telephone with a scrambler. I understand you have one here?" The Inspector nodded and said he would have to go and get the key for room 25.

"Can you wait for two minutes? I'll be right back. You'll be in contact with your superiors straight away. Emergency, is it? I hope it's not what I think it is?" and so saying he hurried off.

Tom dialled the number and Inspector Ferguson waited close by. "Hello! Can I speak to the highest officer on duty please?" He waited a moment and then said, "Major Brownlow, this is Lieutenant Davidson speaking. I am on active service in Northern Ireland and I am anxious to find out if our security has been breached. My direct superior is Captain Darcy and I am concerned that there is a dramatic increase in the numbers of active, quality subversives in our district. I believe they have now drawn down weapons and are closing in on one of our operatives. I need you to check with Captain Darcy. See if he is available to return my call. This is urgent. I am at the RUC station in Enniskillen." He hung up.

For half an hour he paced the room and talked to Inspector Ferguson. He was very agitated. Finally the telephone rang. The Inspector answered it and then passed the receiver to Tom saying, "It's Colonel Heaps!"

The Colonel told Tom that Darcy had not reported at 1900 hours, neither at 2100 hours. By 2300 hours he had not returned to base.

"I think," said Tom, "that a major breach of security has occurred and would need to be debriefed. Please send a helicopter for me to go to Thiepval and later on to Cheltenham. Thank you." He turned to Inspector Ferguson, "It looks bad for Darcy!" he said.

My God, man!" said the Inspector nervously, "you guys are in a very dangerous game!"

"Yes," said Tom thoughtfully. "When I left Belduff, three active Provisional IRA men were closing on my colleague who is living in a caravan park – Lieutenant Dickson. I am frightened for his life. I feel I may have just escaped with mine."

VIII

Heather woke up early on Saturday morning, for a change, and lay in her bed wondering why. Suddenly she grinned, remembering that she had a date with Gilbert. She yawned, stretched, pulled her pillows down and her blankets up around her chin and shoulders and, snuggling down luxuriously, she thought about what she would wear that night. She settled for her mini pleated skirt and black top and decided that she would go and get her hair done in the afternoon. She tried to go to sleep again, failed and so got up and dressed.

Gilbert phoned her at lunchtime. "Hi Heather!" he said, "everything all right for this evening?"

"Yea, grand," said Heather a little breathlessly on account of the anticipation.

"I'm going for a jar in Henshaw's before the hop. Will you meet me there?"

"That'll be fine," she said. "What time'll I meet you?"

"Say about ten?" he said.

"That'll do rightly," she answered. "I'll see you then. Bye."

* * *

Olive glanced up from the book she was reading as Heather came into the living room. Putting a bookmark between the pages she closed the novel and put it beside her on the table. "You look lovely, darling," she said approvingly. "Do you think you'll be warm enough? I hope you have a good evening. Don't be too late and drive carefully. Need I state the usual rule?"

"No Mum," said Heather resignedly. Then she quoted her mother – "No matter what time you get home, come and tell me you're back!"

Olive smiled, then standing up she kissed her daughter. "Goodnight my chicken!" she said.

Henshaw's was packed with young people loudly sharing the week's happenings. Friends sat in groups, couples sat very close to each other with the newly-matched among them appearing a little awkward. Young macho men made the most noise and were almost equalled by the prettier self-assured females. The people behind the bar sweated profusely while they pulled pints and filled orders, and the television, turned on in the corner, was ignored by all except those who wished to know the sport results. Henshaw's was a young person's bar. When dance time came it would empty very fast.

When Heather strolled in, Gilbert, who had been watching the door, stood up and waved to her. Making her way gingerly among the tables and the waving hands holding pints, she came up to him and sat down on the stool he had been minding for her. She nodded greetings to his friends, some of whom she had known at school, and then Gilbert called a passing barmaid and ordered her a drink. "I'm just drinking Coke," he said, "but please don't let that put you off drinking whatever you want." Heather was not put off at all. She drank beer. They yelled at each other above the noise. Chiefly they yelled about how she was getting on with the Greenfinches and then it was time to go to the hop. Gilbert said, "We're as well to walk to Parklands. Sure it's only a few hundred yards. We'll leave the cars in the car park here. They'll be quite safe."

Outside the weather was nippy and Heather shivered. Gilbert did not let the chance pass and quickly put his arm around her shoulders. Heather stiffened slightly and hoped that no one she knew was watching her. Ever since the episode with Archie she had avoided, as far as possible, any close contact with men, young or old. But she wanted to get over this. She wanted to be able to discuss boys and dates and kissing – and more – just like the girls with whom she had been to school. She didn't want to be different from them. So when they got inside the dance hall and there came a slow dance and Gilbert began to dance close with her, she steeled herself and got on with it. She loved music and dancing. Henshaw's beer was going slowly and pleasantly to her head and she relaxed. Gilbert kissed her neck, nibbled her ear and then searched for her lips with his. She turned her head away and Gilbert gave up. Gilbert was a bit of a gentleman on the dance floor.

Hand in hand they walked back to Henshaw's car park. Heather wondered if all she now had to do was to thank Gilbert for a lovely evening, but Gilbert decided for them that the night was not over. He led her towards his car saying that he knew a fine quiet spot where they could go and talk. And Heather, for all her misgivings, was inquisitive. As her heart beat oddly, she remembered overhearing a conversation that she well knew she was not meant to overhear. She had been passing the open living room door on her way to bed and, Aunt Thelma, sounding exasperated, had been telling Olive that sex in her marriage was dead. Olive suggested that Thelma should be patient. Thelma said, and Heather remembered it verbatim, "If I get it once a month I'm doing well. For God's sake Olive, I'm not expected to sit on it until the maggots get it am I?" Heather did not wait to hear more and tiptoed quickly up the stairs.

Heather got into Gilbert's car and vowed she'd try this thing that Aunt Thelma found important in her life – if she were to be given the chance.

Gilbert drove some miles out the road and into a wood. "We come here on manoeuvres," he said proudly. "It's very quiet." Music from the charts was playing on his radio.

"I love this one," said Heather, stalling.

"So do I!" said Gilbert putting his arms around her and planting his lips wetly on hers. Heather protested a little, but knowing that no one was there watching her she became submissive. Gilbert was gentle. She realised that. She allowed him to run the tip of his tongue around the inside of her mouth and was amazed to find it quite thrilling. Gilbert found it thrilling too. She forced Archie from her mind by thinking of what she could tell the girls, and Gilbert put his hand between her legs. She gripped her thighs tightly together so Gilbert took his hand away and also took his arm from around her shoulders. He sat and stared out the window. "Do you not want this Heather?" he asked.

Heather swallowed before saying in a small voice, "I think I do."

"Well then," said Gilbert, "can I let your seat back?" He leaned over and pulled the lever so that Heather fell back, her feet on the floor, staring up at the roof.

"Oh dear God," she thought, "now what!"

Gilbert fumbled with his jeans and she heard him undo the buttons one by one. "Take off your tights and pants!" he whispered.

Heather felt mortified but she did as she had been asked. She put them neatly on the seat behind her. He pulled his jeans down and she took a furtive look and saw the whiteness of his bum gleam in the darkness. She also saw his erection. "This," she thought, "is going to be awful."

Gilbert reached for her hand and put it gently on his penis. "Stroke me!" he begged. She did and she felt the slippery moistness on the top of it. He pulled her skirt up and caressed her clitoris. She was embarrassed to realise that she too was moist. Gilbert was breathing strongly through his nostrils and when he leaned over her she could feel that his heart was pounding. "Oh God!" said Gilbert with passion, "I love you!" and wrenching her hand away he launched himself on top of her. "Please, please," he urged, "open your legs." He took his penis in his own hand and searched with it for entry. Heather did not help. He found home. He thrust once, he thrust twice. Heather held her breath. He groaned, "I'm going to come!" and he pulled himself up off her body, grabbed his glistening penis and ejaculated on her belly while propping himself up on his left arm. Deftly he got over the gear shift and threw himself back onto his own seat and panting said, "Christ, I'm sorry!" He pulled his jeans back on and offered her his handkerchief. "There," he said, "dry yourself with that and get your clothes back on. I'd better get you to your car. Your mother will be wondering what's kept you."

Heather was rather shocked. She dried her stomach and handed him back the sticky mess without saying anything. She asked him to put the seat back the way it was and then she reached into the back for her clothes. She put them on. All this time Gilbert was looking out the window. When she had finished he said, "OK?"

"Yes," she said. He put his arms around her and gave her a kiss on the cheek.

"You're great," he said. And that was it. He started the engine, turned the car and when they were out on the open road he took her hand. "Can I see you next Saturday?" he asked.

"Yes," said Heather thinking that she was as well. Sex, she surmised, is a queer thing, and she was puzzled that there was so much talk about it. She couldn't think why Aunt Thelma found it so necessary. But she was now, at least, one of the gang and she had a boyfriend.

She reported in. Olive was awake. "You're a bit late dear," she said doubtfully.

"I know Mum, I'm sorry. But Gilbert and I sat talking for ages. You know how it is!"

"He'd be Jim and Mary Watson's son, wouldn't he?" asked Olive. "Yes, I remember him. He's a nice lad. Good night darling. Sleep tight!"

Heather went to bed but she couldn't sleep.

* * *

Dessie, Mick and Tom walked steadily up to the mobile home in the caravan park in Belduff. Almost simultaneously they hammered on the door and burst in. The red-haired man who was sitting at the table inside was completely taken by surprise.

"Lieutenant Dickson I presume?" said Mick. "Up on your feet!" he snapped. The man pushed his chair back and did as he was told. Mick went on, "I am arresting you on behalf of the Chief of Staff of the Provisional Irish Republican Army. Move away from the table!" The man moved and, as he did so, Mick pulled a revolver with a silencer from his pocket and shot two bullets calmly into each of Dickson's knees. "Like James Bond, no one escapes us you know! Who is your boss, as if we didn't know?"

The man gasped, "I am not this Lieutenant Dickson you speak of. You are mistaken! I am Pauric Gallagher."

"Tom," said Mick, "this gentleman is not listening. Get the blocks! He's intent on making this hard for himself."

Tom, taking Dessie with him, left the caravan. While he was gone, Mick watched the mental and physical contortions of the counter-terrorist then said, "We have your boss, Captain Darcy, in custody you know. He has given us your full details – your PAYE number, your date of birth, your service at home and overseas."

"No!" said the man, "you're lying!" and he groaned. He closed his eyes and listenend while Mick correctly listed all of the stuff he had said he knew. Tom and Dessie returned and dropped the breezeblocks on his legs. The man was tough and it took a long time before he finally broke and gave the names and information needed by the men. Then they shot him.

* * *

A gillie, Thomas McGowan, was waiting at an angling pier on Lough Melton when Lieutenant Dickson's body arrived for disposal. The driver asked him, "How the hell will you keep him submerged?"

"That's no problem at all," said the gillie. "I'll take him out to near Bilberry Island and then I'll put weights on him and drop him over the side. I'll fish there with my clients for the next three weeks or so. The Sonaghan and Gilaroo will feast on him and clean him up for us."

"There'll be a few others to follow. You were told, weren't you?"

The gillie nodded. "I'll be ready," he said.

* * *

Miley Cadden drove his taxi straight from Enniskillen to O'Moore's Bar and met the boys. "I dropped Tom O'Donnell off at the Coin Bar about midnight," he said. "Said his sister was ill and that he was going to visit her. He also said that he would see me tomorrow."

* * *

"Jesus!" said Dessie, suddenly remembering Roisin, the barmaid from The Warrior Queen, "What about the women and the disco!"

Mick and Tom smiled. "Yea," said Tom, "what's your hurry? There's plenty of time. We'll get to see them all right. Business comes first!"

* * *

At about that time, Lieutenant Davidson, alias Tom O'Donnell, was making a slow descent to Cheltenham. He had a sick feeling in the pit of his stomach that he always got when he sensed that there was bad news. He was right. He was told that with the exception of himself, the whole of G12 was dead. It was assumed that Darcy had broken under torture. Colonel Heaps congratulated him on his vigilance. It was as if the whole operation had ended in an anti-climax for him and he was weary and very sad. Colonel Heaps patted him on the shoulder. "You were lucky to have got out. I have assigned a room to you on the second floor. Have a few hours' sleep and a shower. When you've freshened up come to the canteen. I will debrief you. I'd say we'd have no difficulty in finding the identity of those boyos. A look through the Rogues Gallery of West Belfast should do the trick."

* * *

In the crematorium, Jamieson stood with his colleagues from the office. His mother's funeral service was over. All that was now left of her was her ashes and he was numb. He did not notice Mr Wilmsloe of Consolidated Insurance until he stood beside him and quietly asked him if he would join him for lunch.

IX

The disco, when Dessie, Mick and Tom got there, was in full swing. It was also very crowded. David, the DJ, was justifying his great reputation. His collection of discs was terrific and the way he mixed them drew the crowd. He stood up there above the gyrating mass of humankind, thin as a lathe, head shorn, swaying and mouthing to his music, his earring sparkling and the beads of sweat running down his temples. He loved his job. Now and then he took great gulps from his pint and every so often he would draw deeply from the fag he always kept smouldering in the ashtray by his right hand. He was a hit and he knew it. He'd been about the world a bit, this David, but he always spent the summer months in Belduff. He said he couldn't help coming back.

Dessie spotted Roisin fairly quickly. Her blonde head stood out in the crowd, especially under the strobe lights. She was doing the most amazing things on the floor with a fellow with dreadlocks. Dessie jerked his head in her direction and his mates followed him as he made his way through the sweaty mass, in its continuous state of flux, and tipped her on the shoulder. She shifted her concentration from her rhythmic feet to his face and beamed at him with instant recognition. "So you made it!" she yelled at him above the clamour. Dessie smiled and nodded. He then pointed at the dreadlocks questioningly and Roisin just shrugged her shoulders and walked off the floor followed by the three. The dreadlocks went on dancing. "That fellow's out of it altogether," she said wryly. "Come and meet the girls!"

Over in a corner by the bar sat Sharon and Bridget – both being chatted up by youths who were so full of drink that if they had tilted they would have spilled. Roisin introduced them. She told them that Sharon was a hairdresser and that Bridget worked with horses. Mick ran his eye appraisingly over Sharon. She certainly had the legs just as Roisin had said, but no one had told him about the huge, deep, blue eyes, the unruly black bob of hair and the skirt that was so short that it left him reeling. He rubbed his hands together in readiness for the fray and winked at her. She brazenly winked back but then, noticing that a drunk youth had left his hand on her knee said loudly, "Do you think you can afford that?"

"Afford what?" he said, swaying slightly while trying to focus on the legs that she had stretched out in front of him on a stool.

"Never touch anything that you can't fuckin' afford," she said sassily, gathering her legs to herself.

Completely undaunted he continued, "You must be able to sing?"

"Well, I can," she said, "Why?"

"Because," he said, "you have legs like a bloody lark!"

"Oh Gawd!" she answered quickly, "I thought you were going to tell me I had legs like Tina Turner."

"I don't know who the fuck Tina Turner is!" he said belching. "I have to go for a leak," and he wandered off in search of a lavatory.

"Come on the hell out of this Mick!" said Sharon urgently, "before that git gets back," and the two of them went off towards the dance floor. An older man bumped into Sharon on the way and, full of good humour, said to her, "Sweetheart! Where have you been all my life?"

She stopped and eyed him up and down scathingly and then said with much sarcasm, "I think I wasn't born for most of it." She held out her hand to Mick who was happy to take it and the two of them went to dance.

Bridget, when introduced to Tom, looked relieved. She had had her bellyful of her drunk. As Tom squeezed between the two of them the drunk was saying confidentially to her, "I am a psych-y-atrist at the Mental Hospital in Sligo."

"Well, if that's what you say you are," Bridget said smiling sweetly, "then I am Sharon's manager and she's doing a gig in Castlebar tomorrow night."

"Tell that to the Marines!" said the youth rudely.

"Yes," said Bridget, "and you're not earning much as a psych-y-atrist in the Mental Hospital in Sligo for that hospital is closed you silly bugger! I'm not long left Sligo and I know."

"Shite" said the youth. "I'll have to try again won't I!"

"Well try someone else then," said Bridget kindly. "Come on Tom!" and they too went to dance.

She marched squarely in front of him and he followed her thinking she wasn't anything like as big as Roisin had said, and would be just grand for the night. Besides, horsewomen had a great reputation for being hot stuff.

By now Roisin and Dessie were draped around each other and the lights were dim. David the DJ had relaxed and, as the night grew into morning, the three men and Roisin and her mates willingly allowed lust to overcome them. They left the disco. Guns, blood, breeze blocks, counter-terrorists, hair styles, pubs and stables were forgotten as they lay together in pairs on the headland overlooking Mullan Strand watching the sun make huge, successful efforts to rise over the Atlantic.

* * *

It was a quarter-past-ten on a Saturday night in late October. There was a bit of a gale blowing, and at that hour on a winter's night Kitchiner's Barracks is a desolate place. The Officer's Quarters had just one room occupied. Major Benson, in charge of the platoon, was alone there on night duty.

He sat drumming the three middle fingers of his right hand on his desk. It sounded like a horse cantering very fast. He narrowed his eyes and thought, "Margaret Jackson? No. Not yet. But Heather Elliot seems settled enough."

* * *

Olive, Heather and Florence sat in large armchairs watching television. The library was cosy. The heavy curtains were drawn tight and the large logs burning in the grate threw up little explosions of sparks from time to time. They decided not to turn on the small lamp on the table by Olive's elbow, so the flames from the fire threw shadows on the books which lined the walls. They were watching 'Arsenic and Old Lace'. It was one of Olive's favourite films and as her daughters had never seen it, she had begged them to watch it with her. They hadn't protested. They were good girls and didn't resent spending time with their mother.

Anyway, they were enjoying the film when Florence suddenly sat up listening. "Is that the phone?" she said disbelievingly. Olive reached for the remote control and turned the volume down on the telelvision. It was indeed the telephone.

"Who on earth can that be at this hour of the night!" she said crossly.

"Stay where you are Mum. I'll get it," said Florence, struggling up out of the depths of her chair and running nimbly out of the room and into the icy cold of the hall.

"Shut the door!" yelled Heather, "the draught is fierce." Florence turned back and slammed it. She then went and picked up the receiver.

"Hello!" she said.

"Oh Hello! This is John Benson speaking. May I speak to Heather please…if she is there?"

"Just a moment Major Benson," said Florence politely, "I will go and get her for you." She laid the receiver down and shot back thankfully into the warmth of the library.

"Major Benson for you Heather," she said, throwing herself back into the armchair. Heather left the room.

"What can he possibly want at this hour of the night?" Olive demanded of Florence.

"I dunno Mum," said Florence. "Sure she's not meant to be on duty again until next Tuesday. She told me that last night."

Heather came back into the room looking a bit surprised. "He wants me," she said, "to go on sentry duty tonight. Margaret Jackson can't make it and Mary Lyons, it seems, can't cover for her. So it has to be me. Sure what the hell! I couldn't say no."

"Ah darling, I'm sorry!" said Olive full of sympathy. "But then, I suppose you have to do your duty."

"I'm not bathing again!" said Heather flatly. "It's too damn cold. Good job I have my uniform ready. I'd best go and change quickly. He says he wants me there as soon as possible."

In her bedroom, she quickly changed out of her jeans and sweater and into her uniform. She brushed her hair and deftly put on the beret with the harp on it. She took a quick look in the long mirror at her overall appearance, switched on her electric blanket in readiness for her return and then went downstairs.

"Good girl Heather!" said Olive. "That was quick!"

"I can't tell you exactly when I'll get home," said Heather, checking that all she wanted was in her handbag, "but I will probably be in time for breakfast. He did apologise for giving me such short notice but said I could have a lie-in afterwards! Big deal!"

"He's a tough one!" said Olive nodding. "By the way, I'll be going to early Communion in the morning and when I get back you'll probably be in bed, so take care, my lamb."

"I will," said Heather, going over to kiss her mother on her forehead, "and don't worry about me and church. I'll go to Evening Prayer tomorrow at eight. Bye Florence," she added, "wish I could see the end of the film. Tell me how it finishes."

She drove the five miles of winding road to Kitchiner's Barracks, got out of her car shivering and reported for duty. Major Benson apologised again for bringing her out and sent her to man the sentry box by the front gate. It wasn't very warm in there, but at least it was warmer than outside. There was a Dimplex plugged in in the corner. Heather felt for her gun, checked that everything about her person was as it should be and settled down to sit out her watch.

At eleven-thirty she was surprised to be relieved by Madeline McCullough, who told her that Major Benson wanted to see her in his office.

"Oh God!" said Heather, "what does he want me for now?"

"Haven't a clue," said Madeline, "but you'd better get over there on the double." As Heather closed the door behind her and stepped out into the night Madeline thought that perhaps, after all, she did know why Heather was sent for. Talk was talk, and there was never talk without a bit of foundation. A good job, she thought, that I am plain and getting past my prime. If I were young and nubile like that poor child I might have extra things in this organisation to worry about.

Heather knocked timidly on the door. "Come in Heather!" said Major Benson kindly. "Sit down and make yourself comfortable. It's a bitter night out there and I'm sure you could do with a cup of coffee. The break will do you good."

Heather was puzzled but accepting nonetheless. Over coffee the Major asked her if she was happy in her work and she agreed that she was. He asked after he mother and they chatted on amicably. In was a normal, polite conversation for a boss to have with an employee but Heather felt slightly uncomfortable and didn't know why. When Major Benson left his seat and went towards the door saying, "We'll lock this for security," she definitely felt uneasy. She quickly noted that all the blinds were drawn on the windows. As the key turned in the lock she got to her feet but he was standing in front of her in an instant.

Heather was a lone private. She did not really mix with the other girls and was always at the periphery of conversations. She listened while the others chatted but never really got involved. She had been taught not to listen to idle gossip and had therefore never been included in the chat about the randy platoon leader.

"You find me handsome Heather, don't you?" he said confidently.

"I...I...don't know, Major," she stammered.

"Of course you do," he said quietly. "All you young girls do. I know you chat among yourselves. You love to be associated with power."

"No Major," said Heather in desperation and in a small voice. "I never think about power." She swallowed several times and looked down at the carpet with heart pounding.

He put his hand on her shoulder and she froze. "Come on now Heather!" said Major Benson roughly. "This will only take a minute!" He grabbed her hand and pressed it against his crotch. "You knew why I asked you here!"

Heather began to scream. "You bloody, fucking little bitch!' he hissed through clenched teeth as he slammed the palm of his hand against her mouth to shut her up. While she stared at him with wide, frightened eyes above his large manicured hand he said, "You're the only one who ever objected. Who the fuck do you think you are!" He released his hand and she screamed again with all the strength she had. This time the Major lost his cool completely and grabbed her fiercely around her throat with both hands. He lifted her off the ground and shook her, saying repeatedly, "You little bitch! You little bitch!" Heather fainted and he dropped her onto the carpet. "Now!" he said icily to the cold, ashen-faced form, "you'll get your come-uppance!" and he raped her.

It was all over very fast. Major Benson did up his trousers, straightened his jacket and combed his hair. Cocking his head to one side he looked at Heather with interest and then, having tidied her up too, he dragged her back to the chair and sat her down. He looked at her again and saw that her tights were a bit wrinkled. He knelt to straighten them and as he did so, the girl came to. She stared weakly down at her molester who, sensing her eyes on him said without looking at her, "You fainted, Heather, and if you once open your mouth about what went on here I'll tell my own story. Guess who'll be believed? You are such a little fool." He handed her his comb. "Do your hair!" he commanded. "It's a mess." He went and sat sideways on his desk with his back to Heather, one foot on the floor, the other dangling. With total calm he picked up the receiver of his telephone and dialled a number. After a few seconds he said, "Hello Jill. Could you please go to the sentry box and relieve Madeline McCullough. Tell her I want her to come to my office immediately." He hung up and remained sitting on his desk. He heard Heather put the comb down behind him and he reached back, took it and put it in his pocket. Looking idly around at the girl he said, "Pull your collar up around your neck." As she did this Madeline knocked at the door.

"Come in!" said Major Benson brightly. "Ah, Private McCullough, Private Elliot fainted. The poor girl must have found it too hot in here. Would you be so kind as to take her home and put her to bed. I'm sure that a few hours' sleep will see her right as rain."

Full of concern, Madeline helped Heather to her feet and led her to the car park. "Poor wee Heather," she said. "How are you feeling now?"

"Oh I'm all right Madeline," said Heather weakly, "I'm sure it was just as Major Benson said. Too hot in there."

She's been through the mill in more ways than one, thought Madeline. There'll have to be a stop put to that bastard. And indeed, a stop was to be put on him, but not in a way that Madeline could ever have imagined.

* * *

136

Thelma hummed happily to herself as she sat in her bedroom applying her make-up. She was getting ready to go out to lunch with some members of the Ladies' Committee of the Golf Club. Putting the cap back on her mascara and laying it down she noticed a thin film of dust on the handsome old mahogany dressing table. Wickedly Thelma wrote "Dorcas" in big letters with her index finger in the dust, and giggled because she knew the poor girl would be mortified when she came in to clean there the next day. She tilted her head this way and that while looking at her face in the mirror. She was content. In fact, she was blooming and Patrick Maguire had a good deal to do with it.

Once the make-up was completed the humming turned to singing. "Yesterday," she warbled, "all my troubles seemed so far away..." and then the telephone by the side of her bed rang. Thelma got up from her stool and crossed the room. She made herself comfortable on the side of the bed before picking up the receiver and removing the clip-on earring from her ear for comfort's sake. "Heather, darling!" she enthused, "how lovely to hear from you! Everything all right at home?" She went silent for a time, listening, and an observer would have seen the looks of disbelief and then of anger cross her face. She got to her feet and paced up and down as far as the telephone lead would allow. "Now Heather," she said firmly, "first things first. Please stop crying. We all love you. Never forget that. Not a word to your mother. Is there any chance at all that you might be pregnant? You're right of course, darling! That was a damn stupid question to ask you...Not to worry. I'll be down just as soon as I've peeped into a few little matters, and if there's any reason at all for concern, I'll get things looked after for you. And," she added, "I'll have that hideous, ghastly bastard Benson stitched up before too long. I am shocked by what you've just told me…Just be patient, angel. See you in a few hours. Dry your tears and think how your Aunt Thelma is getting to work on your behalf. That should give you a lift!"

Thelma used her telephone. She spoke to one of the ladies with whom she was due to have lunch and apologised that she could not be there. Double-checking that her husband was not about – she was sure she remembered him saying that he would be out of town that day – she retrieved, from underneath the carpet in her bedroom, the key she had had cut to his study, unlocked the door and went inside.

Well now!" breathed Thelma in the empty room with a satisfied smirk on her face. Who would have thought it! As well as all his disgusting, debauched activities with young girls, Bugger Benson has a woman! He's actually straying! Isn't it the wonder his dick hasn't dropped off! He had some fucking neck to try something on with a member of my family. He'll be sorry he did that!

She took a notebook from her handbag, wrote down a few relevant details and, having turned the computer off and left things as she had found them, she walked purposefully out of the house.

* * *

Patrick Maguire opened his front door to Thelma and welcomed her affectionately. He didn't notice that her taxi had not driven away.

"Jesus!" she said, "Will you give me a chance! I'm not staying. I can't. But I want you to do a job for me. Will you do an important job for me Patrick?"

"Ah God Thelma, don't you know I'd do anything in the world for you. What is it?"

"Well, you can eat the oysters for a start!" she said looking towards them where they lay in splendour on the large plate in the centre of the kitchen table.

"Come on, you witch!" he said, "Out with it."

"You know that newsagent's shop in Belduff? The one with the black front? It has just been repainted?"

"Yes, I've noticed it."

Rooting around in her handbag Thelma said, "Well, I want you to deliver this envelope to the boss – just as soon as ever you can. See that the letter is read while you're there, and get me an answer. Sorry Patrick, but I must go," and she went.

* * *

Patrick drove slowly up the main street of Belduff and when he came to the black-fronted newsagent's shop he parked his car. He felt in his inside pocket for Thelma's envelope, reassured himself that it was there, got out and went into the shop.

He said hello to the thin, positively scrawny woman who stood behind the counter, and commented on the weather. Her eyes watched him and he felt uncomfortable. He put her in her late forties. She was fit. He could tell. "I wonder," said Patrick politely, "if I could see the boss?"

The woman shifted her weight from her right foot to her left and said with a total lack of expression, "I am the boss." Patrick was a little less composed than previously. Producing the envelope and handing it to her he said, "I was asked to give you this and to get a reply." He read the headlines on the newspapers displayed just above floor level while she read the letter.

Looking up she said to him, "I take it you are a messenger – no more?"

"That's it," said Patrick.

"Then," she said, "tell the scribe that we will deal with this in our own time."

"Is that all?"

"Yes," she said and he thanked her and left the shop.

* * *

When Major Benson visited Dot he used to take a taxi to a few blocks from her house and walk the rest of the way to be on the safe side. This affair had been going on for several months and he was delighted that no one had noticed it. As usual, when he was leaving, Dot went outside her front door and looked up and down the street. When she saw that it was all clear she came inside, gave him a peck on the cheek and sent him out, closing the door quietly behind him.

He drew his collar close around his neck and stuck his hands in his pockets before striding up the street in search of a taxi. It was two in the morning. The odd car passed up and down. About twenty yards along his route he saw, in the distance, a woman come out of a laneway and walk quickly towards him. As she drew closer he could hear her footsteps quite clearly. She too had her hands in the pockets of her long coat. She never broke her rhythm. They were the only two people in the street. Major Benson never had a chance. The woman quickly drew a gun with a silencer from her coat pocket and shot him at close range. He groaned just once where he lay on the footpath. The woman, avoiding the blood, stepped over him and walked into the night.

* * *

It was the marching season. Florence asked Heather to go to the village with her to see the Orangemen and Heather said she would. The two of them stood on the side of the street not chatting, just listening and watching. The bands passed by one by one and the sound was familiar, rhythmical and pleasing. The girls found themselves tapping their heels on the footpath, almost unknown to themselves. As the first big Lambeth drum swung proudly past Florence yelled into Heather's ear, "Wouldn't that put you in mind of the Salvation Army joke?"

"I don't remember it," said Heather, "but I am sure you are about to remind me!"

"Yea," said Florence. "The big, busty Salvation Army woman comes over to the group of wee girls watching the performance and says to one of them, "Which hymn would you like, dear?" and the girl says, "If you wouldn't mind, I'd like him on the big drum!" and she pointing at this fine-lookin' young fella."

Florence linked her arm through Heather's and said, "Go on, let you! You can laugh!" and Heather did because she had to. She knew then and there that she really did love Florence.

The Orangemen marched on. Band after band of colour and ribbons, sashes and bowler hats, fine male voices and pride.

Above all there was pride. And the womenfolk stood and watched their men and admired them with their manly chests all puffed out. And they too sang along.

"Oh God!" said the woman by Heather's side with much emotion, "how I love that aul' Sash," and she threw back her head and gave it her all. Heather closed one eye and winced as she bellowed out,
"It is old but it is beautiful, and the colours they are fine.

It was worn at Derry, Aughrim, Enniskillen and the Boyne.
My father wore it when a lad in bye-gone days of yore
And it's on the Twelfth I love to wear The Sash my father
wore."

Along came the next band and by this time the woman had linked arms with her friends, and with Heather, and they were all singing with gusto, "...Oh it's six miles from Bangor to Donaghadee." Florence was giggling helplessly at the enforced antics of her sister. And things continued happily until, looking to her left for the final band to round bend at the bottom of the road, Heather saw with horror the large banner stretching from footpath to footpath which preceded the arrival of the "Cornabowl Kick the Pope Accordion Band." Striding along triumphantly in the lead were two of the most well-known terrorists of Loyalist persuasion.

Certain sections of the crowd cheered until Heather thought their lungs must surely burst. What the marchers sang made her sick, and the closer they got the clearer the words became.
"...Yet the Fenians always try to teach us their ways,
And scorn us for being what we are.
But we want no Fenian Pope or Holy Water,
'No Surrender' is our watch-word near and far.
And if there's going to be a fight hereafter,
And somehow soon we're sure there's going to be,
We'll make the Fenian's blood flow just like water
Down Belfast Lough into the Irish Sea."

She felt the tears swell in her eyes and then burst and overflow down her face. Linked as she was to her neighbour and her sister, she had no hand to swipe them from her cheeks so she let them flow. Shaking her head sadly from side to side, and holding her breath for seconds at a time so that she would not sob, Heather retired into her mind. "It's so wrong. It's all wrong! This is my country and I love it. But every day I meet people who are sick with hatred. How can I stand here and be seen taking part in such an atrocious demonstration of loathing."

As children burst from the crowd and skipped into the road to dance along behind the last band until it reached the finishing spot, she freed her arms and turning to Florence said, "I will never ever go to anything Orange again, never!"

* * *

Heather lay in her bed in the dark. She had no idea what time it was. She was thinking. A dog barked in the distance and the old house creaked occasionally in the familiar way it always did. "Daddy," she whispered into the darkness, "I miss you and I wish you were here. Please forgive me for what I am thinking. I'd hate it if you thought I was letting you down. But I've tried and tried to follow in the family tradition and it's got too much for me. Patrick Maguire believes that if you'd let go of the bloody family tradition you wouldn't have died. I hate thinking about how you went. It wasn't fair. You never deserved that. Mummy and Florence didn't deserve to have you die either, but they seem to be resigned to it and I'm not. They believe you did your duty. I'm not into duty of that sort, Daddy. I'm sick to death of murders and beatings and kneecappings and of no one trusting his neighbour. And all for what? I learnt about

144

Jesus and love in Sunday School. I sang hymns about love. I learnt the Ten Commandments off by heart. I got all the top Sunday School prizes, remember? You were very proud of me for that! I was very pleased with myself. I know I am loved by my family, but why is it different outside of that? I trusted people. I respected them and they were horrid to me. Being different is lonely but I think I have to be different or I'll go mad. Patrick Maguire is a Roman Catholic. He's good, and I know you were a friend to him because he told me. I think he's a friend of mine – the only Roman Catholic friend I have and that's wrong…"

When there was barely enough light coming through the curtains to define the large window in her bedroom, Heather made a decision. She would leave and go to the Mainland. Aunt Thelma would get her a job. There were relations in Lincolnshire who would surely help her settle in. She would give a month's notice to Anna Ormsby, which would be fair. She had not been back to the Greenfinches and refused to let her mind wander back to why. She'd take the little red Datsun with her. She'd miss her mother and sister dreadfully but she would come home as often as possible to see them. She prayed fervently that those two people whom she loved most in all of the world would not think her selfish. With a jolt she realised that Olive and Florence were getting up. She threw back the bedclothes and swung her feet onto the floor. For two seconds she sat on the edge of her bed with her chin in her hands considering, and then she made up her mind that she would go right now and tell them what she had decided to do. "I'll come back," she said firmly, "when all his is over."

X

The rotor blades of the Jolly Green Giant spun and the Chinook rose slowly into the sky. The grass was flattened by the down-rush of air. Thelma waved indifferently with one hand and held onto her hair with the other, cursing because she had had an excellent re-styling job done that morning.

A major security review was taking place at a secret destination in Scotland and her husband was one of the members of the review party. He had just been promoted to Assistant Chief Constable with more money and a bigger and better Jaguar. Whatever about the money, Thelma adored the Jaguar. She felt really on top of the world when she drove it. She loved the way it wriggled its behind when she put her foot hard on the accelerator, and this was exactly what she did as she raced down the M2 on her way to Belfast. She idly switched on Downtown Radio and hummed to herself as she sped along. She admired the panoramic view of Belfast Lough as it lay spread out in front of her.

As she got to the bridge over the Lagan she slowed down. Traffic was building up and she swore at it. Suddenly the music on the radio was stopped for an announcement and the serious voice used for times like this said, "Here is a newsflash. Five minutes ago, a helicopter crashed into the

Mull of Kintyre. On board were most of the top officers of the RUC. It is believed that there are no survivors…"

Thelma pulled over to the side of the road, not hearing the car horns blowing nor noticing the men who gave her the fingers and mouthed, "Woman driver!" She sat there. She felt weak. A patrol car pulled up and a constable came over to her. He knew her instantly, and because he too had heard the news flash, he asked her if she would like him to drive her home. Without a word, Thelma moved with difficulty to the passenger's seat. The distance to her house was covered without one word being spoken. She did not cry. She was not able. The constable understood.

* * *

Thelma did not attend any meetings in Fermanagh for several weeks. She was adjusting to widowhood and spending time with her children. She was also adjusting to parting with the Jaguar. Patrick Maguire was put on the back burner – but she did think about him from time to time.

Patrick, for his part, seldom left his house for fear she would telephone. The opposition gravedigger got four of his graves. The only time he left his house for any length at all was to go to get the weekly supply of oysters – which he ended up eating himself – for he believed that Thelma would definitely know if they had been in the freezer for any undue period. Some days he was so certain she'd call that he had his groceries delivered.

Finally, one Friday she telephoned, and Patrick's relief swamped him. He had barked his shin on the corner of the wooden box of tools he had left in the hall in his hurry to pick up the receiver. Holding onto his damaged limb with both hands and rocking backwards and forwards, he sandwiched the receiver between his shoulder and ear and crooned, "Oh Thelma, how are you! I've missed you so much! How I wish I could have been with you to hold you and comfort you. I tried to phone you but no one would give me your number – not Olive, not the girls!"

"I'm fine, Patrick," she said reassuringly. "Hope you haven't been naughty with those scrubbers!"

"Ah God Thelma!" he said in horror, "on my mother's grave I swear I've hardly left the house since you were last here."

"Right so," she said cheerfully, "I believe you. And Patrick, I'll be down on Monday at the usual time." He closed his eyes when she said this. His cup was full. "You'd better get the oysters!"

"I'll go straightaway!" he said with delight.

"There's no rush," she said, "this is only Friday. And I've decided that I don't like the carpet you have on your bed-room floor. Could you change it for a green one?"

"Of course!" he said, thrilled to do anything that she asked, "anything else?"

"No," she said, "that'll do for now. 'Till Monday then. Bye!"

Patrick put the receiver down and hobbled to the stairs. He pulled his trouser leg up to inspect the damage. There was a bit of grazing and blood on his shin. "Shit!" he said. "I don't think I have any plasters. But Christ, falling over a box for Thelma is well worth it!" He went out to his car to go to the local shop.

* * *

The huge government-owned Zil swept to the kerb and slithered to a halt outside the Kremlin. The door was opened and Colonel Vlad Comorov stepped out smartly. As he did, his breath froze in the icy air to which Muscovites are so well used in winter. He quickly went into the building and straight to his office on the second floor. Closing the door behind him, he went and sat at his desk. He needed peace and time to think out his plan.

Colonel Comorov was the Commanding Officer in charge of counter-espionage in Western Europe. He had held the position for ten years and, up until recently, had found it challenging and rewarding. Now he felt demoralised. He had not been paid for weeks by the Supreme Soviet, and he couldn't imagine when any money would come his way. He was thankful that he had had the good sense to save during better times, but now that little store was dwindling. He cursed the day the decision was made to bring the Revolution to Afghanistan. The mad idiots of the Supreme Soviet hadn't seemed to realise that they were taking on the best warriors in the world – magnificent infantry who would fight this religious war to the death, believing that to die fighting would bring the ultimate heavenly reward. Four divisions had been totally lost and the drain on hard currency severe. Then thirteen divisions of infantry and three divisions of armour were tied up continually on duty. That was no help to the worsening financial situation. As for Gorbachov and the Glasnost business! Comorov shook his head sadly.

He left his desk and paced up and down. Throughout his career he had been trusted for his straight, incorruptible stance. Information he had got that day, together with his feelings of bitterness at having reached the age of fifty-one and being as good as rouble-less, made the thought of defection to the United States very attractive. The more he thought about it the more attractive it became.

Slowly his mood changed from one of bitterness to one of almost glee. He rubbed his hands together and mouthed, "Good man Jamieson! MI5 will be amazed when they find out what you have done!" The files he had on the agents in Great Britain and France should get him all the concessions he wanted from George Lane. His spies had told him that the man was not at all happy in Moscow, so his information could be of benefit to both of them.

Now that he knew what he would do, Comorov began to think about his wife and two daughters. He felt bad that he could not tell them what he was up to. Once in America he would organise a holiday for them in Cuba. There would be a stopover in Shannon where they could seek political asylum. Together the Irish and American authorities would allow them to go to the States. That would work!

"Now!" he said to himself, "let's get George Lane picked up! He'll be out jogging at this time. It'll give him a bit of a fright!"

* * *

While waiting for George to arrive, Vlad Comorov fondly remembered the sun, the warm sea, the Everglades and the Keys along the west coast of Florida. Between the years 1957 and 1961 he had seen action in Cuba and had met Che Guevara. From Lenningrad he had brought one thousand trained warriors and they fought with their guns in the hills and mountains. They finally arrived on the streets of Havana and watched the Americans as they panicked, rushing from the saloon bars and casinos, making their getaway to Miami in whatever way they could. But what he remembered best was the time he had spent with Ronaldo, a young fisherman friend of Che's. They had set out together in a little boat, strongly resembling The African Queen of Humphrey Bogart and Katherine Hepburn fame, to go lobster fishing, and had ended up going all the way to Key West to sell their catch. They had smoked Cuban cigars and drunk their way up to Key Largo. He had strutted up and down the boardwalk admiring the wonderful boats moored there, and then Ronaldo had taken him out to see the coral reef and he had been astounded at the clarity of the water and the beauty of the fish and the exquisite formation of the coral. "Yes," he thought contentedly, "Florida is the place for me and my family! It's what we deserve!"

George Lane was the CIA'a Head of Station, Moscow. It was the most important post of its type in the world and he was proud of himself when he was given the appointment. It meant a big hike in his salary and his expenses were enormous. Moscow was a great listening post and these were exciting times with the beginning of the collapse of the Communist system and the withdrawal by the Russians from Afghanistan. It was the first reversal the Red Army had had since its ignoble retreat in front of the Blitzkreig in the Second World War. This was a change from Langley in Virginia where he had been teaching Russian, amongst other things.

He had always kept himself fit by jogging each morning, but jogging in this infernal cold was more of a chore than a pleasure. On his way home to his apartment he trotted into Lennin Avenue and was more than surprised when a large Zil drew up beside him and two sergeants got swiftly out. George Lane halted, panting, and the men came to stand on either side of him. "You will please come with us," they said, ushering him into the car.

Comorov's office door was opened and George Lane was shown in. He looked puzzled. After the two soldiers had been dismissed Vlad Comorov turned to him and smiled. "Sorry to bring you here like this but it was necessary to avoid suspicion. Would you like a cup of coffee? Americans always drink coffee, isn't that so? We Russians prefer black tea."

George Lane was pleased to accept the coffee. He needed liquid of some sort after his exertion in the severe cold. When it came it was hot, sweet and strong and Comorov benevolently watched him drink it. He was the king pin in his plan for defection and he was delighted to have him in his office. They made small talk for a while, but the minute the coffee was finished and the cup put back on its saucer, Comorov said to George Lane, "I wish to defect!" Lane's face was impassive. Comorov continued, "I am prepared to bring relevant files with me. I am sure you realise that they will be of great benefit to you?" Lane nodded. "These are my conditions. I want a house in Florida with comfort and security, a Colonel's pension for life and a lump sum of three times the annual salary. I know how you can get me out." He waited while George Lane considered his own position. He was not happy in Moscow. If he could pull this one off, he would get promotion and, with any luck, a transfer back to Langley. His wife, Penelope, had refused to go with him on this assignment. She didn't speak Russian and said firmly that she did not want to move the children out of the school where they were happy. He was lonely without them. This information had to be big stuff, for this man was in charge of Russian espionage in the UK and in France and had a clean reputation.

"OK," he said to Comorov who was sitting on the edge of his chair enthusiastically waiting for his decision, "I'll go for it! I can sanction your defection here and now."

Comorov sat back in his chair and relaxed. He locked his fingers together and rested his chin on them watching the American. Finally their eyes met and they smiled, each of them knowing that what had just passed between them was to their mutual advantage.

"Right then," said George Lane, "my man will meet your man in the tea shop on Lennin Avenue at 1500 hours on Wednesday?"

"Yes," said Vlad Comorov, "everything will be in order." They discussed their agents, how they looked and what they would be wearing, and finally they agreed on the exchange of words.

* * *

Nikita put the brown paper parcel and his newspaper under his arm and looked at his watch. Because it was twenty minutes before three o'clock and there was plenty of time, he decided to go on foot to the teashop. He easily lost himself in the crowd of depressed people who walked the streets of Moscow on that very cold day.

In the tea shop he looked around, spotted whom he believed to be his man in the left corner at the back, got his cup from the counter and walked towards him. He was reading his evening newspaper, Vechernyaya Moskva. After excusing himself and asking, in Russian, whether it would be all right to join him at the table he said in English, "What was the temperature in Miami yesterday?" to which the man replied, "How hot would you like it to have been?" Everything was, as Comorov had said, in order.

* * *

154

The very next morning, Comorov hugged his wife that little bit tighter as he kissed her goodbye before leaving for work. He felt that today would be the day. He hoped everything would go well, but he had been long enough in the job to know that plans went wrong sometimes. He would love to have told her what he was about. What he did do was to go to the door as if to leave, then he turned and came back to where she stood and taking her in his arms he whispered, "Love of my life!" and then he went. Mrs Comorov got the faintest whiff of a rat.

* * *

The American dacha was warm and welcoming when Vlad Comorov reached it. (All the clothing he had was what he stood up in. When George Lane told him that Headquarters were anxious to have him on board as their employee he tidied his office and left.) He had not thought about food for hours and was glad to find that the hospitable Americans had thought of it for him. He ate well and patted his stomach contentedly. He felt really chuffed that he had got his information in first. He knew that there would be mass defection soon, as the current spate of secrets began to be sold. He was the lucky one to have had first access.

He was given an overnight bag and some clothes and told to go and change. While pulling on his trousers he heard the blades of a helicopter begin to rotate and immediately felt sorry that he had eaten so much. He could still be turned back by Air Traffic Control or, worse, be shot out of the sky. He swallowed and squared himself, took a look in the mir-

155

ror, patted a bit of stray hair into place and, saying goodbye to his Russian clothes and his Russian life, left the room.

The helicopter pilot was waiting for him. "We're on schedule, Sir," he said, "but we want to keep it that way so let's go!"

As Comorov hurried after him he said, "Is George Lane not coming with us?"

"No, Sir," came the reply and Comorov thought to himself, "He's wise. If I were in his position I wouldn't attempt to leave with a defector of my kind either!"

"You understand, Sir," said the pilot, "that we are flying fairly low so as to remain undetected by Russian Air Traffic Control?"

"Yes, but where are we going exactly?"

"We have big enough fuel tanks on this baby to take us all the way to Oslo, after that you will transfer to a regular flight and go to Washington – and then Langley for debriefing."

"Ah," nodded Comorov, "I see." He closed his eyes and vehemently wished himself out of Russia and into safety. He thought that he would have been sent to London first, but then London was not to be trusted any more what with Burgess, Blunt, McClean and their ilk. "MI5 is riddled with buggers like those," thought Comorov contentedly, "but my favourite is the fellow Jamieson!"

Finally the pilot told him with relief that they had left Russian air space and then there was conversation between the two of them until they reached Oslo. Comorov told how he had ordered four defectors shot out of the sky in his former existence. He then explained that he could now see all of this from a different perspective – and the two men laughed at the irony of it.

In Oslo, Comorov went through duty free and spent the few dollars he had been given at the dacha on vodka and smoked salmon. He was a bit sick of caviar. He boarded his plane and sat beside a serious career woman who designed kitchens. He did his best to be interested but was relieved when she went to sleep.

Crossing the Atlantic was a piece of cake after the helicopter ride. In Washington, Comorov was transferred to a small aircraft and was taken on to Langley where he was welcomed by the assistant chief of staff of the CIA. He was told of the arrangements for his security and then advised to go and have a good rest before his debriefing on the following day.

In his apartment, Comorov was suddenly overcome with loneliness. Strange country, strange people, strange surroundings, no wife, no daughters – he took out his clean, ironed white handkerchief, shook it open and blew his nose loudly. Then he dabbed at his eyes and finally he cried, just a little.

* * *

Mrs Whicker was extremely concerned by the delicate information given her by her Cabinet Secretary. The problem was, just who was she to trust? She was disillusioned at that time. "Snooty-nosed, pedantic idiots the lot of them," she sniffed. "Tons of intelligence yet no common sense. What I must do is keep a tight rein on all this information, improve on my listeners, sort out my Red-leaning civil servants and give them a good boot up the arse.

Buckingham!" she yelled through her open office door. "Get the Deputy PM on the telephone and tell him to get here fast!"

The Deputy Prime Minister arrived running and was told not to eat or even go to the lavatory, but to get himself immediately to Northolt. Being used to Mrs Whicker, he understood what he was to do pretty quickly.

The Deputy Prime Minister of Great Britain flew from Northolt to Washington. He went to collect the relevant files that Comorov had spirited from Moscow. He spent only a few hours on American soil before flying home to London with the documents under seal for Mrs Whicker. Jamieson was in deep trouble.

XI

Thelma stood in the centre of Patrick Maguire's kitchen, her hands on her hips, her feet planted on the floor and decision chiselled all over her disapproving face. She was about to make an announcement. Patrick knew the signs. He sat at the table waiting for the outburst. His calm infuriated her.

"Patrick Maguire," she began, "you're going back to university to finish your studies. I will be the laughing stock of Royal Belfast if the lady golfers ever find out that I am having and affair with a part-time grave-digger." She paused, waiting for a response. She got none. Patrick looked at her steadily and with interest. Squaring her already squared shoulders indignantly she raised her voice a tone and went on, "You're an intelligent man and will have no trouble getting your degree. You've told me that you have a photographic memory and, into the bargain, you retain everything and recall facts easily." Again she paused. Again no response. Thelma was getting cross and flushed. "When you qualify," she said curtly, "you will have an earning capacity of over fifty thousand a year. I just know that you will finish top of the heap!" As she reached for her handbag which was lying on one of the kitchen chairs she said, "It just so happens that I have here in my bag all the forms needed for you to do as I say." Spreading them in front of him and offering him a pen she said, "Just sign here, and here and, oh, here as well. I've marked the places.

Patrick did not take the pen. He straightened himself against the back of his chair, crossed his legs easily and said, "Thelma, my sweetheart, I know that what you have in mind for me is, in your opinion, for the best and thanks for all the trouble you have gone to. But now you've got to think of what I'd like. I won't have my career and future possible earnings dictated by the feelings of the sporting lady golfers of Royal Belfast. I know that a woman of your standing can't possibly have her photograph taken with a part-time gravedigger and it put in the Ulster Tatler! I'm not a complete eejit Thelma! I'll have my own method of making my way up this social ladder that worries you so much. I'll do it by investments and a bit of business. We can go into this together for all that. I've been checking the businesses for sale for the past little while. Did you know that?" He didn't wait for her to reply. "For all you found out about me off your late husband's computer, you didn't get the whole of it. The money I got for the farm is in a safe little spot just waiting to be used. It'll break my heart to sell this house, but for us I am prepared to do that. I'm told it's worth about thirty thousand. Putting all I have together, I think I could afford a small hotel in a village in west Donegal you know. That's what I have in mind now!"

Relieved to have off-loaded all his plans onto this woman, Patrick Maguire uncrossed his legs and leapt to his feet. Gathering the startled Thelma in his arms he swung her round and round, humming "The Homes of Donegal" into her ear. He then whispered wickedly, "What I have in mind my crazy spearbhean, is much better than going back to college." She tried to struggle free of him and say something, but Patrick Maguire was big and strong. Like Rhett Butler in Gone with the Wind he carried her up the stairs, laid her gently on his bed, reverently covered her body with his and kissed her with all the passion he possessed.

* * *

"Excuse me, Sir," said the sergeant as he hopped out of the police car and stopped Jamieson in his tracks. "I am sergeant James Jones. I am attached to Marylebone Police Station. This is my warrant card. Are you Mr Graham Jamieson of 105, Horsham Avenue, Maida Vale?"

"Yes," said Jamieson almost inaudibly.

"I am arresting you for the offence of treason." Jamieson was stunned. "You are not obliged to say anything but if you do choose to speak, what you say will be taken down and may be used in evidence at your trial. Put the cuffs on him Danny!" he said, tilting his head in Jamieson's direction. Dazed, Jamieson was obliged to go down the wide stairs between the two men. In the street a Ford Granada was parked with the engine running and the back door wide open. Passers-by stopped to stare and put their hands to their mouths as Sergeant Jones got into the car first, followed by the traitor and his minder. The door slammed and as the car sped quickly away towards Marylebone they looked at each other in amazement and then began to ask each other what it was all about.

In the police station the reason for Jamieson's arrest was explained to the duty officer. "Right!" he said, "now empty your pockets!" Slowly he put his loose change, his wallet, his pen, his penknife and his handkerchief on the table. He behaved like an old, old man.

"Come on!" urged the Duty Officer. "Your watch now!" Jamieson stared at his possessions while a clerk listed them in a book and then he wrote his signature at the bottom of the page. He found it difficult to control the pen.

Before he was led away, the Duty Officer said, "You have been charged with the very serious offence of treason against the realm. You will be questioned . Do you wish this questioning to be in the presence of your solicitor?" Jamieson nodded. "You are allowed just one telephone call."

"Yes, I want to call Abraham Grundy," he said. "My solicitor."

* * *

Mrs Imelda Gillespie was flustered.

As a teenager she had been courted by John Gillespie and things had taken their usual course. They married when she was twenty-one and he twenty-two. Things were difficult at first but then John got a good job managing the local farmers' co-operative, and in the space of five years they were blessed with three sons. "That's enough," thought Imelda. "Things will be clean and decent from now on in." So she swapped the double bed for two singles and got on with rearing her family. She did suggest moving to another room but John said that it wouldn't be necessary. She looked after her maiden aunts, Agnes and Martha, and she was rewarded well by them. They left her the Lobster Bay Hotel in Portnafarraige, a tiny village in north-west Donegal just a few miles from where she and John had set up house fifteen years earlier.

Having sold the house, the family moved into the hotel and Imelda Gillespie put her heart and soul into building it up into the fine enterprise it was now. John continued with his own job. It provided the bread and butter in the early years and he was happy at it.

The county of Donegal took off as a tourist destination and Portnafarraige, settled in the crook of an Atlantic cove, became a mecca for those seeking a healthy, peaceful holiday on the western seaboard.

During famine times, hungry men were put to work building a harbour in Portnafarraige in exchange for food. It was a beautiful structure with a big, robust wall to keep the little cove from the buffeting waves and winds of the Atlantic. It used to harbour only little fishing boats that were used by the locals to catch mackerel or drop lobster pots. Now it was also home to the larger yachts of the wealthy who came from Dublin at weekends.

The Lobster Bay Hotel was just above the harbour on the other side of the road that ran through the village and around the hill in a semi-circle. The road then straightened out to meet itself again. The hotel was two stories tall, long and pretty and flanked by charming little houses on either side. "Cosy" was the adjective often used to describe it. The view was incredible. There was the vast Atlantic to the front and the Donegal hills to the rear. It was a veritable paradise.

Imelda had her finger on the pulse of all that was happening in tourism. Where there were grants to be had she had them. She extended the hotel to the back, put in extra bathrooms, enlarged the dining room and found herself a good chef who specialised in seafood. The rest of the staff was local, and during the school holidays her sons did their fair share of the work. She was pleased when her eldest decided that when he left school he would make a career of hotel management. Imelda's cup was full until the awful day when John came home and told her that he had been promoted. This promotion would mean moving to County Carlow.

Imelda deliberated. She tossed and turned in her single bed at night. She agonised over everything – leaving her dentist, her doctor, Donegal, her home, her hotel, her husband. John remained unmoveable. In the end she went to confession.

"No, my good woman," said Father Flanagan. "As a practicing Catholic, you must stay by the side of your husband. To expect him to come home to you at weekends is out of the question. You must go with him. For the good of your marriage and your family the two of you must stay together." He blessed her, and she went home and advertised the Lobster Bay Hotel in The Irish Times, The Irish Independent and also in the Donegal Democrat.

* * *

Thelma and Patrick Maguire drove to Portnafarraige after lunch one day towards the end of September. They had an appointment with Mrs Gillespie. The nearer they got to their destination the narrower the road became. As Thelma took her foot off the accelerator and changed down into second gear to get around the final corner she said, "This had better be good, my friend, because it's a real bitch of a road to get here!" Patrick sat comfortably beside her enjoying the magnificent scenery. Suddenly the village of Portnafarraige was in front of them and Patrick felt an exciting tingle of anticipation as he looked down on the Lobster Bay Hotel. Thelma found a well-worn space by the side of the road and pulled over, leaving the engine of the car running. She took a deep breath and said, "Looks like it could be the item all right." For a few seconds they sat side by side in silence absorbing the beauty, and then Thelma put the car into gear and they went on down the hill and parked in front of the hotel.

"Would you like to freshen up before having a cup of tea?" asked Mrs Gillespie kindly. "You've had a long journey."

"Yes, I'd love to use your loo!" said Thelma, but let's leave the tea until after we've seen around."

Thelma insisted that they see everything from the cold room to the broom cupboards. "Now show us the books," she said.

As Mrs Gillespie rattled on about twenty-two bedrooms with bathrooms en suite, the annual turnover, the kitchen that had been recently inspected and passed by the North Western Health Board, the fine state of the fire escapes, the six months of Saturdays which were completely booked for weddings, her orderly tax returns and her reason for selling, Patrick Maguire, who was totally disinterested in the conversation, was gazing at the sun. It was setting like an enormous half orange over the sea. He loved the place. He wanted it. He didn't care right now for the silly details. What bothered him was the price and whether or not he could afford it. He wished Thelma and Mrs Gillespie could come to the point. Suddenly he became alert as he heard the owner of the hotel say, "The price is two-hundred-thousand pounds." He looked at her steadily. He was wondering if he should say that he would have to think about it. Thelma quickly seized the moment and said sharply, "We'll give you one-hundred-and-seventy-five. Take it or leave it!"

Mrs Gillespie thought fast. It was the best offer she'd had. "I'll take it," she said. "You can have possession in sixty days."

* * *

"Well Patrick, anything to report since the last time?" said Thelma flinging her coat onto a kitchen chair in such a way that it immediately slithered off onto the floor.

Patrick bent to pick it up saying, "No Thelma. It's as boring as Churchill's 'dreary steeples'."

"Why are you studying me in that funny sort of way?" she asked him. "I was once forced to read 'A Portrait of the Artist as a Young Man' by James Joyce. I was told it would do me good. It was a paperback and there was a photograph of him on the outside and he was looking at something in the same way as you are looking at me now."

Patrick grinned. "I read that same book myself. I know that cover. The fellow who took it asked Joyce what he was thinking at the time and he said, I think, that he was wondering if the photographer would give him a few bob!"

"And are you wondering if I would give you a few bob?" she retorted while raising a well-Tabascoed and lemon-juiced oyster to her mouth.

"No," he said, "I was wondering if you'd marry me." By the time he'd said the last word Thelma's head was tilted back and she was sucking in the oyster. She brought her head down to look at him and the juice dribbled from the corners of her mouth. She slapped her lips shut, swallowed the oyster, wiped the juice away with the back of her hand and said, "Jesus I could have choked!"

Patrick burst out laughing but Thelma was serious. "You're some prick my old Sharpening-stone!" she said affectionately. "I do love you but to marry you would be right out of the question."

"Ah," he said, "I suppose it wouldn't suit the sporting ladies of Royal Belfast!"

"No," she said coming over to put her hands on his shoulders and look into his eyes. "No, it's not that at all. There's the fact of your religion. I think it would split the family and I couldn't have that." He was about to speak but she interrupted, "Please believe me. I love things the way they are. I'm really looking forward to visiting you weekly in Paradise in Donegal. I love spending time with you. But to marry you…No!"

She stood back from him and his gaze was on the floor. He was deeply hurt. But down in his soul he knew that she was right. It wouldn't work.

"You wouldn't be thinking of telling me to fuck off or anything like that?" she said, anxious to break the silence.

Looking at her fixedly he replied, "I'm as well to tell you the rest of what wasn't in your husband's files I suppose."

"What!"

"I'm a Sleeper."

"Oh Dear God!" she cried, "and to think that I didn't know ·that! What am I to do! Jesus!"

"What are we both to do Thelma;" he said sadly.

They stood far apart, looking at each other. Now they could think of nothing to say.

* * *

Daffodils are hardy flowers. No matter how many people are murdered, or how dreadful the political situation, how deep the pain in the heart, or indeed how harsh the winter, they bloom again when their time comes around. Olive Elliot sadly but lovingly arranged the daffodils that she had picked in the jug with the long neck.